Two weeks alone with five children?

The very idea terrified Julie. Helping out with parents nearby was one thing, but handling things alone would be an entirely different matter.

What if one of them got hurt or became ill? What if she became sick? Every possible negative scenario played through her head.

Stop it. You're a capable woman—able to handle any and every thing thrown at you and more. Well, not everything. She hadn't dealt with Noah's desertion.

The thought gave her a moment's pause. Was his presence the real reason she didn't want to go? Seeing him daily while knowing how she felt about him would be difficult enough. Knowing she would have to walk away again and never have him in her life made it nearly impossible. Could she withstand the pain it was sure to cause?

TERRY FOWLER is a native Tarheel who loves calling coastal North Carolina home. Single, she works full time and is active in her small church. Her greatest pleasure comes in the way God has used her writing to share His message. Her hobbies include gardening, crafts, and genealogical research. Terry invites everyone to visit her webpage at terryfowler.net.

Books by Terry Fowler

Christmas Mommy

Terry Fowler

Heartsong Presents

To my family. Writing this story reminded me of the good things that come of being part of a large family.

Special thanks to Tammy and Mary for your help.

A note from the Author:
I love to hear from my readers! You may correspond with me by writing:

Terry Fowler
Author Relations
PO Box 721
Uhrichsville, OH 44683

ISBN 1-59789-038-3

CHRISTMAS MOMMY

All scripture quotations are taken from the HOLY BIBLE, NEW INTERNATIONAL VERSION®. NIV®. Copyright © 1973, 1978, 1984 by International Bible Society. Used by permission of Zondervan. All rights reserved.

All of the characters and events in this book are fictitious. Any resemblance to actual persons, living or dead, or to actual events is purely coincidental.

Our mission is to publish and distribute inspirational products offering exceptional value and biblical encouragement to the masses.

PRINTED IN THE U.S.A.

one

It's not that hard."

Julie Dennis almost laughed as she admonished her brother, the pastor. "Shame on you, Joey. You know it's wrong to fib."

"I'm not. It's not," he insisted.

She leaned back in her chair to search the files on the cabinet behind her, never pausing in her work. "Maybe not for you and Mari. You're old hands at this kid stuff. I don't have your experience."

"Please, Julie. This trip is a lifelong dream of ours. Something we could never afford."

His statement caused Julie pain. She hated it when Joey dropped bombshells like this. How many times had she told them that if they needed or wanted anything they only had to ask? "Why didn't you say so?" she demanded. "I would have paid for it."

"And we'd have the same dilemma," he reminded.

"I don't mind staying with the kids. That's not the problem."

"I know. The timing could be better."

Julie agreed wholeheartedly. "No joke." She tapped the keyboard and the screen saver clicked off. After finding the information in the folder, she keyed the data and smiled when the programming problem solved itself. "Who goes off and leaves their kids at Christmastime? That's the most unbelievable thing I've ever heard."

"It's not really Christmas," Joey said. "And the kids won't even miss us. Having you around, spoiling them outrageously, will be tons more fun than having us here."

Her brother's attempt to sweet talk her fell short. "Yeah, right. Laying it on with a trowel is not working here."

"Mari promises to write long, copious lists. You'll be able to handle this blindfolded with one hand tied behind your back."

"You think I'd try that with those kids of yours?"

Joey ignored her comment. "You should hear Mari. She's more excited than I've seen her in a long time."

He wasn't playing fair. No doubt, Mari was ecstatic at the thought of going somewhere without the children. Julie loved her brother and sister-in-law but found their literal interpretation of "go forth and multiply" somewhat embarrassing. Her friends could hardly believe they'd made her an aunt five times over with five-year-old Matthew, four-year-old Marcus, three-year-old Lucas, and fourteen-month-old twins John and Naomi.

"She needs this trip."

Julie noted the concern in his tone. "She's not. . ."

"She's fine," Joey reassured quickly. "Back in her full-time role of wife, mother, and pastor's wife, but she's lost her sparkle."

A breast cancer scare on top of her mother's death would depress any woman. "She's been through a lot. You need to take some of the load off with the kids."

Joey sighed. "I try but Mari says her job is to keep me free to handle my pastoral duties."

"What about putting them in day care during the week? I'd be happy to pay the fees."

"Use of the church day care is one of the benefits of the position, but Mari says she's a stay-at-home mother for a reason. She refuses to put the kids in day care for more than a few hours at a time."

Julie admired her sister-in-law's ability to organize her family and home. The model homemaker, Mari ran their home like a well-oiled machine. Not only did she cook fabulous meals, she kept a spotless home and they had five well-behaved children. And she managed to work tirelessly with Joey in the church.

Maybe that's what really made her nervous. Julie knew that if she said yes, Mari would find that her efforts to train her sister-in-law in the fine art of homemaking had failed. No doubt, the place would be in total chaos within hours of their departure.

"Noah's willing to help."

The mention of his name caused a stab of pain in Julie's heart. She didn't think she could bear seeing Noah daily. *That would be worse than the kids,* Julie thought.

"I understand, Julie."

Maybe Joey did understand that the idea of caring for his kids all on her own terrified her, but he had no idea how she felt about Noah Loughlin. The overwhelming sense of abandonment she'd felt when Noah relocated to South Carolina to accept the position of associate pastor at Cornerstone Church still bothered her.

Noah and Joey had met at seminary, and when he set them up on a blind date, claiming Noah was perfect for Julie, she decided to reserve her opinion. Instead, she found Noah to be handsome and personable and fell into "like" almost immediately.

When Joey's family moved away, Julie had leaned on Noah and he'd helped make the separation bearable. Then in May, Noah's out-of-the-blue announcement that he'd taken the associate pastor position took the wind out of her sails.

Julie had never thought she'd miss Noah so much. Only after he'd left had she realized how much she loved him. But Noah had never indicated he wanted more than their casual relationship.

Still, she'd considered the idea of relocating to South Carolina a time or two before Joey had casually shared how popular Noah was with the women of the church.

Evidently, he'd moved on and she decided she had to as well. Even now, Noah's presence played a major part in her relationship with her family. The thought of seeing him gave her reason to keep fifteen hundred miles between them most of the time. On the rare occasions when she traveled to South Carolina, she tried to avoid him as much as possible.

When Noah called, he acted as if nothing had changed, but Julie knew everything had changed for her. She refused to be involved with a man who couldn't be bothered to seek her opinion when it came to making decisions that affected them both.

"At least pray over it," Joey requested, bringing Julie back to their conversation. "If you can't see a way to do this for us, we'll understand."

Sure they would, Julie thought with a grimace. For the rest of her life they would have long faces and sad stories about how they would have visited the Holy Land that time if things had worked out for them. "I assume Noah's already agreed to take over at church?"

"He's looking forward to this opportunity."

He would be, Julie thought. "You mean he doesn't rate a free trip?"

"The church didn't give us the trip," Joey explained. "Friends found they couldn't go and gifted us with their nonrefundable tickets. You'll find having Noah around will be a great help. The children adore him."

"Maybe you should ask him to babysit while you're away."

"Mari insists on family."

"Just my luck," she mumbled under her breath.

"Did you say something?"

Julie coughed. "Okay, Joey, you win. I'll see what I can work out."

"You already said you were coming for a couple of weeks. And we'll be home to spend Christmas Day with the kids. I promise not to say anything about the expensive gifts you buy, either."

That almost made it worthwhile. Julie couldn't understand why Joey could never accept her gifts in the spirit they were intended. "What about the kids' Santa?"

"Mari plans to do the shopping before we leave."

Obviously, no stone would be unturned once the wheels were in motion. "I'll let you know. Tell everyone hello for me."

"I will. Julie," he called when she started to hang up, "I don't mean to pressure you. Asking you to care for five kids is a major favor."

You're telling me, Julie thought. "Joey, I love you, Mari, and those kids with all my heart. You know I wouldn't refuse you anything any of you asked that's within my power to give, don't you?"

"I hoped that would be the case," he admitted, his big laugh making her homesick. "We love you, too."

❧

Noah could see his arrival had disturbed Joe's deep concentration. "You were lost in thought," he commented as he sat in the visitor chair.

Joe grimaced. "Suffering from guilt pangs. I suspect I just coerced Julie into babysitting for us while we're away."

Noah doubted that. Julie never stopped looking for ways to repay her brother for what he'd done for her. She'd see this as a prime opportunity. "I doubt you coerced her."

"We know we're taking advantage, but I don't know where else to turn. Mari needs this break."

"Julie does know I plan to help in every way I can?" When Joe nodded, Noah asked, "You don't think she would refuse because I'm here, do you?"

Noah felt his friend's scrutiny.

"She's already planned two weeks' vacation over the Christmas holiday. Why would you think that, anyway?"

Noah's gaze zeroed in on Julie's image in the photo sitting on the credenza behind Joe's desk. Her blemish-free complexion and chocolate brown eyes gave her a youthful, innocent beauty that struck Noah in the pit of his stomach. He missed her so much.

Taller than the average woman, she stood somewhere around five foot ten and longed to shed those final twenty pounds that would take her to a size six. She frequently finger-combed her thick, shoulder-length brunette hair back from her forehead.

"She's become very good at avoiding me," he admitted glumly. "I haven't talked to her in a couple of weeks. I keep getting her voice mail."

Joe frowned. "Why would she ignore you?"

Noah leaned back in the chair and crossed his legs. "I wish I knew. I thought everything was moving along smoothly. I believed Julie—actually, I've started seeking God's guidance in regards to asking her to marry me."

"You're that serious?"

Joe sounded surprised. "I am. I don't know how Julie feels, though. I believed we were both serious but now that she's barely speaking to me, I don't know what to think. She's been distant since the move. You think that's the reason?"

"Probably," Joe said. "My sister puts on a brave front but she's afraid. I had a real struggle leaving her behind. I've been her guardian since our parents died. At least I had them during the hard times. Now she doesn't have anyone."

"She still has you."

"Not as accessible," Joe declared. "I asked her to come here, but she says it's our time to be a family without her breathing down our necks. I have no idea why she feels that way. Mari and I love her a great deal."

Joe's thoughts intrigued Noah. Maybe her brother could give him some indication as to why things had changed. "Do you really think she's afraid?"

"I hear it in her voice at times," Joe admitted. "Sort of a little girl sadness, almost as if she's close to tears. But I don't see it when she's visiting. She seemed fine when the twins were born and when she came to help after Mari's surgery. She doesn't say much about us moving away anymore."

"I wish she'd tell me what's on her mind," Noah said.

Joe's hearty laughter echoed around the room. "In your dreams, buddy. Women believe the men they love should be capable of reading their minds. I've learned to listen carefully to what Mari says so I don't end up in an argument."

"Julie won't tell me anything," Noah declared. "When I told her God called me to Cornerstone, she told me to do what I had to do. What kind of comment is that?"

"Women's logic?"

"I'd hoped she'd be as happy for me as I was for her when she got her promotion at work."

"Had you expressed any intent toward her?" Joe asked curiously.

"No. I felt God was telling me to give her time. She's young and I don't want to rush her into marriage too soon."

"It's a good idea to take your time and seek God's guidance in choosing your helpmeet," Joe advised. "Even if I do know Julie has excellent values and morals and is a generous and loving woman. Of course, I admit to a slight prejudice. Would you like me to pray with you?"

"Please."

The two men bowed their heads, seeking God's guidance in the matters of the heart.

After Joe finished praying, Noah thanked him and the conversation turned to the business of hospital visitations.

❧

Two weeks alone with five children? The very idea terrified Julie. Helping out with parents nearby was one thing, but handling things alone would be an entirely different matter.

What if one of them got hurt or became ill? What if she became sick? Every possible negative scenario played through her head.

Stop it. You're a capable woman—able to handle any and every thing thrown at you and more. Well, not everything. She hadn't dealt with Noah's desertion.

The thought gave her a moment's pause. Was his presence the real reason she didn't want to go? Seeing him daily while knowing how she felt about him would be difficult enough. Knowing she would have to walk away again and never have him in her life made it nearly impossible. Could she withstand the pain it was sure to cause?

Joey had said Mari needed the trip. Was there something he wasn't telling her? She didn't think so. No doubt, there were aspects of their lives they didn't share with her, but they'd always shared the major problems like Mari's cancer.

Her brother's determination to give his wife this vacation surprised Julie. While Joey wasn't as clueless as some men were when it came to women, he'd never struck her as the romantic type. Julie agreed that Mari would benefit from the trip. In fact, she would be the first to say Mari deserved a vacation.

She opened the calendar on her PDA. She'd already requested the week before and the week after Christmas. How would her boss react to her adding another week? *No time like the present to find out,* Julie decided as she picked up the phone and requested a few minutes of his time.

She left Kevin's office fifteen minutes later with her plans approved. As it turned out, he had already planned to give everyone an extended holiday break.

Julie liked her boss. After graduating at seventeen, she had gone off to college with the intention of getting her bachelor's degree as soon as possible. She'd chosen computer engineering, and during her college years her instructor's high praises of her abilities had led her to Kevin Moore.

He'd offered her a part-time job and she'd worked hard to help him design the business software programs. When she graduated, the position became full time.

Her brother and sister-in-law sold Julie and Joey's parents' house after Joey accepted the Cornerstone position. Julie had used part of her share of the money for a down payment on her condominium and invested the remainder in Kevin's firm.

The investment had been a wise one, and with her generous salary, Julie lived a debt-free life with considerable savings in the bank.

Julie couldn't help but wonder what role Joey's prayers had played in Kevin's decision. The Lord worked in mysterious ways.

Once she completed the projects on her desk, her calendar would be clear until after New Year's Day. Julie decided not to mention that third week to Joey. If the situation overwhelmed her, she might decide to head for home as soon as Joey and Mari returned. Julie had no doubt she could appreciate the peace and quiet of her condo after a hectic two weeks in their home.

Back at her desk, she picked up her cell phone and spoke "Joey's office" into the auto dialer. "You'd tell me if Mari were sick again, wouldn't you?" she asked when he answered the phone.

"It's nothing like that," he said without hesitation. "Mari's depressed. Grieving for her mother and thinking about her own mortality. The cancer scare made her give serious consideration to what would happen to our family if one or the other of us weren't around."

"You think that's why she's insisting on family staying with the kids?"

"Could be. She asked me the other night if I thought you'd agree to guardianship if something happened to us."

"You mean raise the kids?" she asked with a squeak of fear in her voice.

"Don't panic, Julie. It's not going to happen."

"But it could."

"If God sees fit to take us from this earth, I know you'd willingly accept the responsibility. No matter how frightened you might be, you'd provide the children with the love and guidance they need. I assured Mari I didn't doubt it for a minute."

Her brother's confidence in her shook Julie to the core. She'd never once considered the possibility of raising his children. As far as she was concerned, Joey and Mari would still be around when their great-grandchildren were born.

"That's the sort of melancholy I'm hoping a vacation will alleviate," Joey told her. "Having you here taking care of the kids will reassure her considerably."

"Okay, Joey, I'll be there for Christmas," Julie agreed despite her reservations.

"I can't thank you enough, Julie. We'll call tonight to finalize the plans. Mari will be so happy."

Julie could tell Mari wasn't the only one. Joey sounded excited, too. "I'd say you owe me a big one, but it's no more than you've done for me."

"Because I love you," Joey said.

"Because I love you back," Julie responded in their usual exchange. "Tell Mari to list where she gets her endless supply of patience. I'll need to order a double batch."

"That one's easy, Jules. It comes from God."

"Then you'd better start praying now."

"We both should," Joey suggested.

two

Julie refilled her coffee cup and leaned against the counter beside Mari. "Are you excited?"

"Yes and no," her sister-in-law admitted. "I've dreamed of going but I'm torn over leaving the children. I know you'll take good care of them, but I worry people will think I'm a bad mother."

"We both know that's not true," Julie said, her thoughts going back to the scare of the summer when Mari found the lump. Julie had come to stay with them for two weeks then, helping care for the children and forcing Mari to take it easy after the surgery.

Even that had been a struggle. If she laid down for a nap, more often than not one of the kids slept with her. Despite the protests of her husband and sister-in-law, Mari always rose early to prepare meals and stayed up late doing chores. Nothing stood in the way of Mari spending quality time with her children.

"I'm not as worried about the older boys as I am the twins. I'd take them along but they'd be the only children," she said, bringing Julie back to the present.

"Exactly the reason they need to stay here with me. I'm looking forward to spending time with the twins. I promise to cuddle them as much as you would. And I'll call right away if there's any emergency."

"You're wonderful to do this for us," Mari said, tears clouding her bright blue eyes. "Not only did I find the love of my life when I married Joe, I got the sister I always wanted."

Julie opened her arms to Mari and they embraced. "I don't want you worrying. Think of it this way—you'll both be better parents after a little break. I plan to keep them so busy they won't have time to miss you. Well, maybe just a little," she teased at Mari's playful frown.

"Naomi, no," Mari called, going over to stop the child's efforts to escape the high chair.

Julie caught a glimpse of Joey and Noah as they carried the suitcases out the front door to load them in the church van.

Noah looks more like a cover model than a minister, Julie thought. Standing over six feet tall, he wore his executive suit with a flair that most men could never achieve. His olive-toned skin gave the impression of a permanent tan and suited his short black hair and gorgeous doe-brown eyes. He laughed at something Joey said and stole Julie's breath away.

"I bet he packs the church," she said softly. "I mean. . ." Julie stuttered and looked at Mari. "I'm sure Joey does, too."

Her sister-in-law chuckled. "Neither of them does badly. Julie, Noah told Joe he thinks you're avoiding him."

She focused on the bottom of her coffee cup. "Why would he think that?"

Mari stepped closer and wrapped her arm about Julie's shoulder. "Joe and I don't want to interfere. We want you to be happy. Do you love Noah?"

Julie glanced at the front door, afraid the two men would return in the middle of their conversation. "I don't know what I feel. Or what Noah feels for that matter. I just know I don't want a long-distance relationship."

"If you care for him, why would it matter?"

Julie knew she couldn't tell Mari the truth. After Noah had left, she'd decided she'd spent far too much of her life without the people she loved. While Joey had worked hard to take care of her after their parents' deaths, he hadn't been her father and mother.

Just about the time she'd begun to feel settled with him and Mari, she'd graduated from high school and started college. They had two children and one on the way when she graduated. Julie had insisted they remain in the family home and gotten an apartment. She'd seen her family on a regular basis and felt content. When Luke arrived, she'd bonded with the infant. Then they moved to South Carolina.

Julie remembered the day Joey called to ask her to stop by the house so they could share their news.

"The beach, Joey?"

He'd laughed at her disparaging question. "The Grand Strand, Jules. Sixty miles of sandy shore, blue skies, and water."

"You sound excited."

"We are. You know Mari and I have been praying for God to lead us where we can do the most good. I'm confident Cornerstone Church in Myrtle Beach, South Carolina, is exactly that place.

"Mari and I looked on the Internet and found it's listed as the best family beach. The kids are going to love the area. They have amusement parks, miniature golf courses, and plenty of family entertainment shows."

"A nice place to visit, maybe, but who'd want to live there?"

"We do. Warm hospitality, small town feel with a population of twenty thousand."

Julie had glanced at the literature he'd handed her. "That swells to over 350,000 during the summer season. Come on, Joey, it's named after a shrub."

"Give it up, Jules. We're going. We'd hoped you'd consider coming with us."

"You mean move and live there?" When Joey nodded, she'd said, "No way. My life is here. My job, the condo, Noah."

He'd raised his hand. "Okay. It's just a thought. I've looked after you so long I suppose I'm suffering from separation anxiety."

"Then don't go."

"We have to, Jules. This is what God wants us to do."

She'd found herself hoping they'd experience a change of heart, but when Joey asked if she wanted to keep the house, she knew they were serious.

When Noah followed them, Julie knew without doubt that she couldn't handle another loss.

"I'm not into long-distance relationships," she told Mari. "I need to see the man in my life more than once or twice a year."

"Will having him around be too much for you?"

Mari's concern posed yet another problem. If Julie admitted the truth, her sister-in-law would refuse to go on the trip. "We'll be okay."

Julie hoped that would be the case. She planned to spend as little time in Noah's company as possible. Of course, she already had her doubts that would happen. She'd come downstairs this morning to find him waiting in the kitchen. He'd kissed her without hesitation. Surely he didn't think they'd pick up where they left off when he'd abandoned her.

After Joey and his family had moved, she and Noah had seen each other nearly every day. He knew exactly how much she missed her family and yet he'd chosen to follow them rather than stay with her.

Granted, she knew Noah had to follow God's leading, but the least he could have done was show a bit of hesitation over leaving her. He'd been so joyous about his job opportunity that Julie wondered about his eagerness to escape her.

"This isn't the end, Julie Joy," Noah had said that last night as they held hands over the dinner table. "It's a beginning."

His cryptic words puzzled her. How could it not be the end? Maybe she would have followed him to South Carolina if he'd asked, but he hadn't. Instead, she remained behind to deal with her love for him, and that had been no little task.

Julie recalled their conversation earlier in the week. She'd been on her way out when the phone rang. Her mind had been on her errands and she'd grabbed the phone without checking the caller ID.

"Hello, Julie."

"Hi, Noah. I'm on my way out the door to complete my errands before I fly out day after tomorrow."

"Why don't you want to talk to me anymore?"

"Don't be ridiculous," she'd told him, more than a little aware he'd hit the bull's-eye with his guess.

"I don't think I am. This is the first time we've talked in two weeks. I miss hearing your voice."

"I've been busy getting everything organized."

"Joe told me you're coming. I can't wait to see you."

Had he honestly thought her so gullible that she'd believe him without reservation? "I'm sure you'll be far too busy in your role of associate pastor."

"Are you saying you don't want to see me?"

"We'll see each other, Noah."

"But do you *want* to see me?" he'd persisted.

What had he expected her to say? That she looked forward to as well as dreaded seeing him? That she feared one glimpse might undo her determination to move on with her life without him? "Sure I do."

"You could sound a bit more enthusiastic. It seems like forever since you were here."

"Nearly six months. Right after you accepted the position."

Ironically, not quite two weeks after Noah moved, Joey called to ask for her help. Julie had traveled to South Carolina only to find she and Noah were too busy to spend time together.

"I have so much to tell you. I want to hear everything you've been doing, too. I can't wait for you to meet our church family."

"I've already met most of them. Mari keeps me current."

"You must talk to her fairly often."

"Once a week or so."

"Why don't we talk that often? You call Joe and Mari but you can't find time in your busy schedule to talk to your boyfriend?"

How could she have told Noah she was far too angry with him for idle chitchat? Too afraid to hear how quickly he'd moved on in his new life without her? "We play lots of phone tag, Noah."

"Because you're never around to take my calls. I miss you so much at times that I dial your number just to hear your voice."

Julie had choked up at his words. If only she could have believed that. "Can we decide who's at fault later? I really do need to run my errands."

"Okay, Julie, if that's what you want."

His tone set her on edge. "What I want is to stay warm and cozy in my house, but I have to find Christmas gifts for the kids."

"Why can't you buy the gifts here?"

Julie sighed at his obvious inexperience. "Because it takes away the surprise element when they see what I buy for them. Besides, it's easier to shop alone. I'm going to have the packages shipped. I can't imagine getting on a plane with all this stuff."

"How much stuff?"

"There's a pile of boxes in my living room," Julie told him. "I am buying for seven. . .uh, eight people."

"You can send everything to the church. I'll sign for the packages."

"Thanks, but most of the stuff won't arrive until after I'm there anyway."

"What else can I do to help?" he'd asked. "Pick you up at the airport?"

She'd already had this discussion with Joey. Julie planned to rent a larger passenger van and drive herself to the house. "I've got a passenger van reserved at the airport. We're going to cover Mari's list after I get there."

"Sounds like you don't need me."

What could she have said? She didn't want to need him.

"It's going to be hectic. My plane doesn't take off until around noon Sunday and I have two layovers."

"Take care, then. I'll be praying for a safe journey."

They had not spoken again until this morning. Julie had caught them up on the community they'd called home for years and her work. She'd listened to their news, and Julie realized that in just a few minutes, Joey and Mari would share their last-minute instructions before Noah drove them to the airport.

"It's cold out there," Joey said, blowing on his hands as they came through the kitchen door.

"You think that's cold?" Julie asked. "You should visit me more often. Your blood is thinning out."

Joey placed his chilled hands against her neck and she squealed and moved away.

Noah followed Joey, his cheeks rosy red. The boys congregated around his legs, vying for his attention. "Mari and Joe are happy you're taking care of my partners here."

Julie picked up three-year-old Luke, who'd fallen after Matthew and Marc pushed him out of the way. "We're going to take care of each other, aren't we, guys?"

The three boys nodded.

Noah rested his hands on Matt's and Marc's shoulders. "Feel free to call on me anytime. I've gotten to know these guys over the past few months."

Mari opened the cabinet door and took down two mugs. "Since Noah's covering for Joe, he won't be able to go home to his family for Christmas."

"That's a shame," Julie said. She believed in family holidays. No matter how busy her schedule was, she always made time to spend Christmas with her family.

Noah cupped his hands about the mug Mari handed him and sipped the hot coffee. "I don't mind. Joe and Mari deserve a vacation."

"He's joining us for Christmas dinner," Mari announced,

passing Joey a cup of coffee. "I wrote notes about the plans for dinner, what to buy at the grocery store, what to take out of the freezer and when."

Julie smiled at that. "Perfect. Lists are my life. I can handle anything as long as I have a good set of instructions to follow."

Mari's loving smile filled Julie to overflowing with good feelings. "I know you'll do fine. Joe and I can't tell you how much we appreciate this."

"Consider it a cheap Christmas present," she joked.

"Oh, you," Mari said, tapping Julie's arm. "I'd better check upstairs one last time. I always feel I'm forgetting something."

"Leave something behind," Joe told her with a grin. "There's no room in the van."

After Mari left, Joey and Noah talked church business and Julie watched John feed himself. He abandoned his spoon and ate the cereal with his fingers. Fighting back the desire to assist, she noted his mother had given it to him dry and put his milk in a sippy cup.

When he indicated he was finished, Julie wiped his mouth and took him out of the high chair. She set him on his feet and watched him toddle into the living room where the rest of his siblings played.

Being in Joey and Mari's home was almost like being in her parents' home. The table they'd dined around had been in the senior Dennises' home for most of her life. The same furniture her parents had chosen for their living room sat in Joey's living room.

Joey had insisted that she take some pieces for herself. Julie had kept her bedroom suite and a corner curio that now contained her own and her mother's pottery collections. She also had a set of bone china that had belonged to her great-grandmother. She'd insisted they needed the rest of the furniture more than she did.

After depositing the dishes in the sink and wiping off the

high chair tray, she glanced at her watch. "It's almost time, Joey."

He stood and walked around the table, his hands gently massaging her shoulders. "I'm glad you're here, Julie. Perhaps the kids and Noah can get you into church a couple of Sundays."

Julie caught Joey's gaze and shook her head. Their ongoing argument about her failure to attend church regularly happened every time they spoke on the phone or saw each other. Joey just didn't understand the demands of her career. It wasn't that she had forgotten her religion. She just didn't have the time or desire to attend church.

"I'm sure Noah doesn't want to hear this." Embarrassed that Joey had dragged him into their argument, she glanced at Noah and said, "Joey still thinks of me as a child."

Her brother frowned. "I know how easy it is to get away from God and church, Julie. You promised you'd go back."

"Drop it, Joey." He wasn't responsible for her any longer. Though she appreciated the way he'd taken care of her since their parents died, Julie wanted him to admit she was a responsible adult.

One of the children cried out and Julie went into the living room to check on them. Joey and Noah followed.

"You should have arrived earlier and attended services with us yesterday."

His criticism stung. She'd been dead-tired when she pulled into their yard around eight o'clock last night. "I restructured my entire life to be here. Isn't that enough?" she demanded.

Joey remained steadfast in his determination to get his point across. "You can never give me a good enough reason for not attending church."

Mari came downstairs and handed her carry-on bag to her husband. "Joe, please," she requested softly, touching his arm. "Julie understands your concerns. It's between her and God."

"All I'm asking is that she attend church."

"And she will," Mari said patiently. "Julie knows what she needs to do."

"That's right, Joey. I'm an adult capable of making my own decisions. And for the record, I didn't come earlier because we had our company Christmas party Saturday night and I was expected to attend." Fuming, Julie took a couple of steps away from the group, still muttering her arguments. "I rush around all week to be with my friends so I can come up here and keep his kids and that's the thanks I get."

Mari came over and hugged her. "We do appreciate this, Julie. More than we can tell you. You two need to kiss and make up. I don't want this vacation spoiled because my two favorite people are angry with each other."

"I'm not angry with her."

"I'm not angry with him," Julie said at the same time. She walked over and hugged her brother. "I promise to go to church while I'm here."

"I suppose that's better than nothing," he agreed reluctantly.

"Good," Mari said, wrapping her arms about the both of them. "We'd better talk to the kids one last time before we go."

Julie's heartbeat kicked into overdrive. They were about to grant her wish to be treated like an adult. Once her brother and sister-in-law said good-bye to their kids, she would be in charge of five small children. What was she doing here? Why had she agreed to their plan?

Having a few friends over for a small party was her biggest Christmas achievement. How would she turn the next ten days into a joyous occasion for her niece and nephews? At least John and Naomi were too little to warp with her failure.

"Boys, we want to talk to you," Mari said.

They are so cute, Julie thought as they assembled to hear what their parents had to say. Matthew, the oldest, was destined to be a lady-killer with those big blue eyes and jet-black hair. At four, Marc was the quiet one. He came and stood within the circle of his mother's arms, not really listening as Joey outlined what they expected of them. Three-year-old Luke was the independent one. He sat on the floor, making truck noises and pushing ruts into the carpet with his dump truck. John toddled over to the toy box and proceeded to throw things out. His twin, Naomi, watched a television commercial.

"Aunt Julie will be your mommy until Christmas. I expect you to listen to her and behave," Joey said firmly. The older boys nodded while Luke continued to play. "Do you understand, Luke?"

The little boy nodded solemnly and said, "Auntie Hulie Christmas mommy."

The adults smiled at each other. Julie swung Luke up and playfully nuzzled his neck. "You're so sweet. I could eat you up with a spoon."

Luke squealed. "No eat, Auntie Hulie." She put him down and he went back to playing.

"You may wish you could before we get home," Joey warned. "Luke is our, ah, determined child. You have to be firm with him."

Joey pulled his oldest son into his arms. "Matt, you're the oldest. You help Auntie Julie. You guys know your mother and I will not tolerate bad behavior." He glanced at his sister. "Aunt Julie will punish you if you misbehave."

Julie panicked. That wasn't part of the deal. She couldn't discipline these children. "I never. . . I can't. . ."

"Yes, you can," Joey told her firmly. "You're the adult in charge." He spoke to the children once more. "We expect all of you to be very good while we're away. Do you understand?"

Matt nodded. Marc stuck his thumb in his mouth and fixed solemn blue eyes on his dad. Was that a tear creeping down his face?

Joey and Mari hugged and kissed the children one by one, with each "I love you" followed by another reminder to be on their best behavior.

"You're going to have the best Christmas ever," Joey reassured as he hugged Julie one last time. "By the time we get home, you'll be ready to settle down and raise a few of your own."

"Or run screaming into never-never land," she contradicted as she hugged Mari. "Don't worry. We'll be fine."

"You will. Thanks, Julie. You're a lifesaver."

Together the group huddled in the doorway, Marc and Luke hugging her legs while she and Matt waved good-bye. *Any moment now, pandemonium will break loose,* Julie thought, steeling herself for tears.

She experienced a moment's pause when they all went back inside after the van drove away. "Oh well, maybe this isn't going to be so bad after all," Julie said as she closed the door behind her and followed them.

Now where was that list? She found it on the kitchen counter. Back in the living room, she counted heads and settled on the sofa. Mari had kept her promise, listing everything in detail. At least she didn't have to worry about getting any of them off to school early in the morning. His November birthday had kept Matt out of school this year.

Busy with their packing and arrangements, Joey and Mari had not put up the Christmas tree. According to the list, they always got one from the tree farm. *That sounds interesting,* Julie thought. The closest she ever got to tree scent was the times she used pine cleaner in her house.

After she folded over three of the sheets, Julie realized that even though there was a lot to do, she could handle everything she'd read thus far. One day at a time. She laid the pages on the end table and asked, "So what do you guys want to do today?"

"Pway with me," Luke said, coming over to drive his truck along the chair arms and across her legs.

"I like this truck," she said, lifting the sturdy large metal toy as he pressed it into her leg. "Is it a dump truck?"

"Big twuck," Luke insisted.

"It certainly is a big dump truck."

Luke shook his head stubbornly. "Not dump twuck."

Okay, so maybe she wasn't up-to-date on her toys, but it certainly looked like every dump truck she'd ever seen.

Julie opted to sit on the floor with Luke as he ran his vehicle around the carpet. Naomi toddled over with a book and sat down in her lap. She read to the little girl, listening to Naomi chatter in her limited vocabulary. Evidently, Mari read to her children often.

She found having the child in her lap a comforting experience. When she'd arrived the day before, Julie had expected the children to be shy around her because she hadn't seen them since June. They'd immediately showered her with hugs and big sloppy kisses.

Mari had fixed her a sandwich while the older boys fought over who was going to sit next to her. Joey had resolved the situation by telling them they'd have to take turns over the next two weeks. He'd sent them off to play afterward so the adults could talk. Julie had slept on a daybed in the nursery that night.

"Joe and I want you to sleep in our room while we're away," Mari had said as she tucked the babies in for the night.

"This will be fine."

"You'll be more comfortable in a real bed. Besides, I packed all my clothes so you'd have dresser space," Mari had said with a big grin. "At least that's what I'm telling Joe."

Julie had laughed and Mari joined in. She'd move her things into their room before the twins' bedtime tonight.

John came to join Naomi, and one sniff alerted Julie to the need for action before he could sit down. She lifted the twins in her arms and started toward the stairs.

"No!" Luke screamed. "Pway, Auntie Hulie."

His outburst surprised Julie. "Why don't you help me take care of John and Naomi first?"

"Don't want to. Want to pway."

"Play with Marc."

"Want to pway with you," Luke said, his expression crumpling.

"Okay, find me a truck, and we'll play when I return."

How does Mari handle it? Julie wondered as she changed the babies. She cast a doubtful eye on the way she'd pinned on the diapers. First thing she planned to do was splurge and buy some disposables. They would save her time and be much easier than the cloth ones Mari used. She'd even purchase extras for when they returned.

Julie emerged from the nursery with a twin under each arm.

Luke waited on the bottom stair, holding two trucks. "Come pway, Auntie Hulie," he whined.

Julie sat down to play with the three youngest, but within moments it was clear the twins were hungry. "Luke, I have to feed Naomi and John first. Why don't you join us for a glass of milk?"

"Don't want to," came his mutinous reply.

Doesn't he know any other words? Julie wondered as she settled the twins in their high chairs.

She pulled the milk carton from the fridge and searched the cabinets for their sippy cups. She found them in the sink, awaiting washup. Another item for her list.

By the time lunch was over, Julie was more than ready for a diversion. The boys didn't want to play together and when they did, they generally fought over one toy. It took some doing but by two o'clock, Julie had them dressed and secured in the van.

After driving to the superstore she'd visited with Mari and finding a parking space, she ordered the boys to stay in their seats. Julie removed the double stroller from the back and came around to take care of the babies, then allowed the boys to step out of the van.

She pulled Marc's hand up onto the stroller handle and then did the same with Luke. "You boys stay right here in front of me. Matt, take Marc's other hand." Julie locked the van then they crossed the walkway and entered the store.

"No wandering off," Julie instructed once they were inside.

"Stay where I can see you."

She read the overhead signs and avoided the toy aisle. Finding the disposable diapers posed no problem, but choosing the right size was a different matter. After reading numerous labels, she piled three packages into the stroller basket. No sense in running out at the most unlikely of times. She picked up several other items she thought would make her stay easier, including a half dozen extra sippy cups.

"Okay, guys, time to go."

Julie had never felt more obvious than when they moved through the store toward the cash register, catching the attention of more than one shopper.

A rack of sweaters caught her eye and she stopped to sort through them, thinking Mari might enjoy the velvety knits. A squeal caught her attention, reminding her how quickly she'd forgotten the children's existence. Julie glanced around, spotting Matt and Marc playing hide-and-seek in the racks. Where was Luke?

"Luke?" she called, repeating his name when he didn't appear.

"Where is your brother?" she asked Matt.

He stopped running to look around and shrugged. Julie felt the blood rushing to her head. How would she explain losing one of the children on her first afternoon? Where could he be? She'd taken her eyes off him for just a second. *Lord, please help me find him. Please.*

"Luke? Where are you? Answer me."

Her cell phone rang and Julie feared it might be Joey or Mari calling with last-minute instructions. She considered ignoring the ring but desperation won out. "Hello," she called.

"Hi, Julie. It's Noah. Mari asked me to remind you to pick up Marc's prescription. I forgot to call when I got back from the airport."

"I've lost Luke," she cried as she searched the area for the missing child.

"Calm down, honey. When did you see him last?"

"He was right here when I stopped to look at a sweater. Matt and Marc were running around the racks and. . ." Julie gulped back the hot tears that burned her throat. "It couldn't have been more than a minute."

"Take a deep breath. Was Luke running with them?"

"No. I don't know. What if someone took him?"

"Go to the service desk now and ask for help. They'll know what to do."

Julie scanned the area. "I don't see it, Noah. Where is he? He was right here."

"Do you see a store clerk?"

She urged the group a few steps farther, cringing when Marc whined that he was hungry. She didn't doubt it after the way he'd played with his lunch. Feeding him was the least of her worries right now. "No McDonald's until we find your brother."

Luke crawled from underneath the clothes rack. "Pway on swide!" he exclaimed, clapping his hands in glee.

"Daniel Lucas Dennis, you scared me to death!" Julie yelled. "I thought someone had taken you."

His face puckered. "Pway hide seek, Auntie Hulie."

She dropped the phone into the stroller and lifted him into her arms. "Honey, Auntie Julie's sorry she screamed at you, but you have to answer when I call your name. We don't play hide-and-seek in stores."

"He does that all the time," Matt announced.

"Why didn't you say so?" Julie snapped, feeling instant remorse. They were only children. Matt didn't understand how terrified she'd been.

Naomi chose that moment to hurl the cell phone, and Julie dove for it, barely keeping it from hitting the floor. She laid it on her purse in the upper section of the stroller and moved into the checkout line. "Tell you what, guys, let's pay for these things and we'll visit the drive-thru on the way home."

No way was she letting them out of the van again until they

returned home.

Julie urged them forward. Her cheeks flamed beet red when she heard someone calling her name and realized she'd left Noah hanging on the phone. She lifted it to her ear. "You heard?"

"You used his full name. Luke must really be in trouble."

"Talk about conflicting emotions. Does it count that I hugged him after I yelled?"

"Remember what Joe said. You have to be firm with Luke. You have everything under control."

"Just barely. I hope I can keep it together until I get home. I'm not letting them out of the van again until then."

"But Luke wants to pway," Noah reminded, using the small boy's word.

"Not today."

"Better prepare yourself for a tantrum."

"I hope not. I don't think I could handle that on top of his disappearance."

"Respond in love, Julie. Don't do or say anything in anger that you'll regret later."

Was he talking about the kids or them? "When Joey told them I'd discipline them, I didn't realize how serious he was."

"Why would you think that? You've spent time around them in the past. Didn't you discipline them then? Or did you think they'd be angels for you?"

She glanced up to find the clerk watching the boys pile candy on the counter. "I have to go. I'm in the checkout line. Put those back, Luke."

"Don't get upset, Julie."

"Today's been enough to make me rethink the possibility of children in my future," Julie told him as she unloaded her purchases onto the counter, all the while keeping the three boys in her line of vision.

"No way. You'll make a wonderful mother. We'll talk when you get home. Don't forget the prescription."

"Does the pharmacy have a drive-thru?"

Noah laughed. "You're serious about not letting them out of the van again, aren't you?"

"Very."

"I'll run by the drugstore," he volunteered.

"Thanks, Noah. I'll buy you a burger for dinner."

"Make that two. I skipped lunch."

"We should be home within the hour."

"See you around six."

Later, while seated around the dinner table eating their takeout, Julie found herself relaxing a bit. Luke had not misbehaved. He had whined a bit but accepted her one sharp no. Julie suspected he realized he'd pushed her to the end of her rope already.

"I don't think he understands how frightening his disappearing like that was," Julie told Noah after the older boys finished and left the room.

"Luke is willful, stubborn, independent, and cute," Noah said. "Reminds me of someone else I know."

"Stop flirting, Noah."

"Why? Does it bother you? You never minded before."

Naomi tossed her sippy cup off the high chair. Noah caught it before it hit the floor and set it on the table. "You didn't answer, Julie Joy."

Very few people knew her full name. Her mother had been so delighted to have a daughter that she'd given her the middle name of Joy. Joey used it now and again and Noah loved to call her by her full name.

"I don't know. Can we have this discussion later?" she asked when John began to cry.

"Definitely. I need to know where I stand with you."

Julie removed the toddler from his chair and then Naomi from hers. "Come on, kids. Bath time."

"How about I keep an eye on the older boys while you bathe the twins?"

"Okay."

Upstairs, she put Naomi in her crib and took John to the bathroom. The idea of bathing both of them at once made her uncomfortable. Two slippery toddlers would be more than she could handle. Once John was in the tub, Julie found herself so preoccupied with thoughts of Noah waiting to see where he stood with her that she poured baby oil in her palm instead of shampoo. *What a mess that would have been,* she thought as she rinsed her hand in the bath water.

She dried John and dressed him in his nightclothes before putting him in his crib. She wound the toy on the side of his crib and soft music filled the room. Julie lowered the lights before she took Naomi into the bathroom.

How would she keep from telling Noah how upset she was with him? There was no way she'd admit her true feelings. She tucked Naomi in for the night and went to the top of the stairs to call Marc and Luke. Soon all the kids were in pajamas and settled in bed. "Can Noah read our bedtime story?"

Julie called him from the top of the stairs. This house needed an intercom system. "The boys want you to read to them," she said when Noah came into view.

"I'd love to."

They had already picked out the book they wanted him to read. She watched for a couple of minutes and whispered, "I'll be downstairs."

Julie stopped by the nursery to check the babies and found them asleep. She retrieved the hamper from the bathroom and put a load of towels in the washer before going into the kitchen. It surprised her that Noah had picked up the debris from dinner and cleaned the kitchen. He'd even taken out the garbage.

While she waited on the laundry, Julie used her PDA to check her e-mail. "Are they asleep?" she asked when Noah returned.

He joined her on the sofa. "All tucked in, story read, and prayers said. Luke prayed that Auntie Hulie wouldn't be mad at him anymore."

Her heart clenched in her chest. She started to stand. "I should talk to him."

Noah caught her hand and shook his head. "He's asleep. Besides, he needs to understand it's dangerous to disappear like that. He knows you were afraid for him. He learned a lesson today."

Julie dropped back down on the sofa. "Why did I agree to this?"

"You're doing fine," Noah said, taking her hand in his. "You can't let the kids get to you. I know Luke's disappearance frightened you but it worked out. Mari's technique is to divide and conquer. She never takes all the kids anywhere without assistance. If Joe's working, she waits until he comes home and takes a couple with her and leaves the others with him."

Julie slid her PDA back inside her purse and settled back on the sofa. "That's impossible since I'm only one person."

"I'll be your backup."

"Once I convinced myself I could handle this, I jumped in feet first. I don't mind the babysitting part, but I don't want to be the enforcer."

"No one does. But it's part of the job. Children need the love and guidance adults provide."

"It's hard."

He tucked a strand of hair behind her ear. "Just remember you're doing a good thing. Joe and Mari are getting a badly needed break and you're spending quality time with five kids who love you very much."

"I melt every time Luke calls me Auntie Hulie," she told him with a broad grin. "It's so hard to stay angry with him."

"Don't think Luke doesn't know it. He can wrap his mom and dad around his finger, too."

"I've seen you cave in, as well."

"Yep, they're great kids. Wish I had half a dozen just like them."

Julie shook her head. "Not me. Anything more than a couple

requires great patience, and I can't claim an excess of that."

"Okay, do yourself a favor. Lean back and forget the kids. They're in bed for the night. You're free for eight hours."

"More like four. One or the other of them will be awake and needing something by then."

"Relax and don't think about that right now," Noah encouraged, sliding his arm about her shoulders. "Just rest and talk to me."

The dreaded talk. She tensed.

"Something's changed, Julie Joy. I noticed it when you were here this summer. I thought it might have to do with what was going on with Mari. But you've been distant for months now."

"Everything's changed, Noah," she blurted.

Puzzlement filled his expression. "In what way?"

Julie reached for a pillow that lay on the floor. "Seeing you. Talking face-to-face. We spent so much time together in the past that we never had these uncomfortable pauses. I feel them now."

"I don't feel any differently. I can't tell you how much I looked forward to having you here. I've missed you so much."

He obviously didn't have a clue. "Your choice, Noah. You know how I feel about long-distance relationships. You were the one who moved away. Frankly, telephone calls and e-mails aren't my idea of courtship."

"But I thought you understood that I had to follow God's leading."

"Why couldn't He leave you where you were? Joey and Mari followed His leading. Isn't it enough that my family followed His call?" Julie demanded.

"I had no choice. I want to work with Joey here at Cornerstone. I need the experience and he's given me a new perspective which will help when I get a church of my own."

The overwhelming hopelessness that had filled her for months made itself felt. "That's all that matters, isn't it, Noah? Getting your own church."

He shook his head. "No. It's about a future of serving the Lord in the best way I know how."

She couldn't bear the closeness another moment. Julie stood and walked a few steps away. "I thought you were beginning to care about me."

"I was. I do," Noah insisted as he came to his feet.

"Then why is it I feel like I'm at the bottom of the heap in this relationship?"

"I care for you, Julie, but there's an order in my life and God will always come first. Isaiah 30:18 says 'The Lord longs to be gracious to you; he rises to show you compassion. For the Lord is a God of justice. Blessed are all who wait for him !.' "

"What does that mean?" she demanded, exasperated that he'd quoted scripture rather than giving her the straightforward answer she wanted.

"It means we wait on God's timing, not our own. No matter where we might think our relationship is headed, it won't go anywhere without God shedding His grace on us."

"And exactly how does He develop this relationship?" Julie demanded with a scowl of protest. "How can He bless us when we can't even be together because He sent you so far away?"

Noah held her arms and looked her straight in the eye. "Distance is not the problem. God wants to bless you, Julie, but He wants you to exalt and serve Him. Why have you stopped?"

Joey had done his job. Noah had jumped on the bandwagon. She wanted all of them off her case. "I haven't," she denied. "I still believe."

"But you're not interested in serving?"

"I told you I'm busy," she said, refusing to look at him.

A steadfast look of determination crossed Noah's face as he lifted her chin and said, "We all are. Did you ever think that maybe Jesus Christ was too busy to die on the cross for us? For me, there's never enough opportunity to show my gratitude. I need to be in church every time the doors open. And when I'm not there, I should be using my free time to read His Word, pray, and witness to the lost."

"But you do those things anyway. That's your job."

Noah shook his head. "It's more than a job. It's every Christian's calling. When I accepted His name, I committed to become Jesus' disciple. And that means I go wherever He sends me. Never doubt that I wanted to stay with you in Denver, but I couldn't."

Julie spotted some toys the boys had left pushed under the chair. She picked them up and dumped them into the toy baskets. She glanced at Noah. "You've made friends here. Aren't there women who interest you?"

A frown creased his forehead. "Don't you think I'd tell you if that were the case?"

Julie shrugged. "Maybe you didn't know how."

"You don't have a very good impression of me if you think that. When I commit to anything, I'm in it for the long run. I can't be serious about you if I'm dating other women. Do you want to date other men? Is that what you're trying to tell me?"

"No. I miss you, Noah," Julie said softly, staring down at the stuffed animal she held.

"I miss you, too, but it's not forever. Once we work through this our relationship will be stronger."

"How is that possible? I live in Colorado. You live in South Carolina. I see you once or twice a year. That's no way to build a relationship."

"Miles don't matter when you love someone, Julie Joy."

"Noah? I—"

"Don't panic." He advanced and reached for her hand. "Stop running from me. I care for you a great deal and I'm pretty certain I love you."

Julie pulled away. "How can you say that—after the way you abandoned me? You didn't give me any consideration in the matter."

"I did. I do."

"No. You didn't. You walked away from me—from us. I won't risk giving my heart to another person who can't be there when I need them."

Noah appeared shocked by her words. "I had no idea you felt this way."

"Okay, so now you know. What are you going to do about it?" she challenged.

"I'm going to pray for God's guidance—ask what He wants me to do."

Julie frowned. "You've already prayed, Noah. He told you to come here."

"Following God's will doesn't mean you only get one desire of your heart, Julie. He blesses you in all areas of your life."

"I think it's time we called it a night," Julie said, not bothering to respond to that. "The kids get up early."

"I need to know one thing. Do you care for me enough to ask for God's direction in respect to our relationship?"

Julie remained silent as she led the way to the front door. She lifted his jacket and held it out to him.

"Please pray about this, Julie," Noah beseeched as he took the coat. "I don't want to lose you."

"I have prayed, Noah, and I suspect God's told us we're better off apart."

three

Parenting was no easy task.

Julie fell into bed, feeling more tired than if she'd worked round the clock. The minutes passed and she found she couldn't sleep. As if the children weren't enough strain, this emotional tug-of-war with Noah had drained her. She'd been honest with him tonight.

What did she want of him? Would she follow him whenever and wherever God dictated? She honestly didn't know that she could. He'd asked her to pray. She had prayed for peace of mind since the day Noah left her. She didn't want to think about it any more tonight.

Julie fluffed the pillows and located Mari's list on the nightstand where she'd placed it earlier. The number-one item was the tree. If they were going to the tree farm, she would definitely take the twins to the church day care so she could keep Luke close at all times.

How easily he'd disappeared. Almost in the blink of an eye. Goose bumps rose up on her arms. For a moment, the panic she'd felt upon realizing Luke had gone missing paralyzed her. There would be no recurrence of today's incident. Not on her watch.

Julie barely remembered falling asleep before the sound of John's crying woke her. She went into the nursery and took him from the room before he woke Naomi.

"What's wrong, sweetie? Do you miss your mommy?" She filled his sippy cup and settled in the rocker downstairs to cuddle him. Julie hummed softly until he went back to sleep. After returning John to his crib, she headed for the bedroom.

"Auntie Julie, wake up," Matt called, patting her shoulder.

She looked up into three sets of eager eyes. The twins weren't there. No doubt, they couldn't escape the confines of their cribs. "We're hungry."

"Give me a minute to wash the sand out of my eyes."

Luke jumped onto the bed and peered into her face. "How did you get sand in your eyes, Auntie Hulie?"

She held his cheeks and kissed him on the nose. "You ask too many questions, Lukie." She tickled him and he giggled, screaming for her to stop. Soon the other boys piled on the bed, demanding the same.

Julie glanced at the clock and wiggled out of the heap. They were really roughhousing on the bed when she came out of the bathroom. "Okay, guys, I don't think your mom would appreciate you jumping on her bed. Let's get the twins and go downstairs."

Julie had planned a healthy breakfast as she showered. Once she had them all in the kitchen, they frowned at every suggestion. Finally, she took cereal from the cabinet and milk from the fridge. The kids seemed satisfied with this so she decided not to sweat the small stuff.

"We're going to pick out our Christmas tree today," she told them as she rinsed juice glasses and placed them in the dishwasher. "Let's get dressed." She instructed the boys to brush their teeth.

They made a great deal of noise as they ran up the stairs.

"Your brothers are too loud," she told Naomi as she removed her from the high chair. The toddler grinned at her.

It took a good hour and a half to get everyone ready. A little less time than the previous day, but Julie wondered how Mari would handle it once the boys started school. She'd have to rise before the sun. On second thought, with her sister-in-law's organizational skills, the change wouldn't cause a blip in their daily schedule.

After delivering the babies to the church nursery, she loaded the boys in the van and checked their seat belts. This would be fun. She remembered the trees of her childhood, the rich scent of fresh evergreen wafting through the house. Strangely enough, as an adult she'd opted to go the artificial tree route, finding it simpler to create the perfect tree that way.

She loved decorating. Every year she searched the after Christmas sales to choose the theme for next year's tree. She had boxes of decorations and everyone always said what a great job she'd done with her home.

Not only would this year's tree be live, she'd planned a major surprise for the kids. While running errands last week, she'd splurged and purchased every cartoon character ornament and light set she could find. She'd even packed them in a box and brought them on the plane with her. Julie smiled in anticipation of their delight.

She checked the map Mari had drawn. It should be just down the road on the right. According to her notes, the owner of the tree farm was a member of the congregation who donated the trees for the church and parsonage each year.

After parking, Julie turned to face the boys. "Okay, guys, here's the deal. I don't want you running off and getting lost, so you have to promise to stay with me. Understand?"

"Yes, Auntie Julie," Matt said, nodding his head.

"Luke, you hold my hand."

The child immediately obeyed her request and Julie relished the comfort of his tiny hand in hers.

They hadn't been there ten minutes before Julie came to the realization that you didn't allow small boys to pick out trees.

"But we want this one," Matt said, tears shining in his brilliant blue eyes. "Don't we, Marc?"

His brother nodded. As Julie's gaze climbed up the pitiful tree, her heart sank. "It's so large. The room's not tall enough. Don't you want to look at the other trees before we decide?"

Matt shook his head. "Mommy would let us have this one."

How could she argue with that logic? Maybe she could cut

off the bottom or something and if they turned the flat side against the wall, no one would ever know. Resigned, she said, "Let's find Mr. Simpson and have him chop it down for us."

"Are you sure, Miss Dennis?" the man asked, confirming her suspicions with his next question. "Is it going outside?"

"No. The living room has a tall ceiling."

His lifted brows expressed his doubt. "It'll need to be taller."

Mr. Simpson was kind enough to drag the tree out to the van. Another tree shopper helped heft it onto the luggage rack. Julie gasped when the limbs completely covered the vehicle.

"We'd better net it," Mr. Simpson said to the man who helped him pull it back down. "She'd get a ticket for sure if she tried to drive home like that."

❦

"Hi. You just missed Joe's call," Noah said when Julie entered the church office. "He tried your cell and then called the church office. Said to tell you they arrived safely. Mari asked how everything was going. I told her you were doing great."

Noah found her smile to be forced. Did it have to do with their talk last night? Noah prayed Julie wouldn't have a closed mind to their future. "Something wrong?"

"No, just sorry the boys didn't get to speak to their parents. I left my phone charging this morning."

She was probably tired, Noah decided. Getting used to kids took a lot out of anyone. "I heard you went tree shopping. How did it go?"

"The tree's on the van. We're going to decorate it tonight."

"That sounds like fun," he said wistfully. He'd bought a small artificial tabletop tree for his apartment even though he wanted the real thing. Pangs of homesickness assailed him at the thought of missing his family traditions.

"You want to help?"

Noah jumped at the opportunity. "Sure. What time?"

"Come for pizza and we'll make it an event."

"Sounds good. Leave the tree, and I'll get it into the stand for you later."

Julie smiled helplessly. "I couldn't move it if I wanted to."

The strange comment surprised Noah, but he quickly put it out of his mind. "Oh, I almost forgot. Joey said they couldn't call too often. Said it costs too much."

Julie sighed. "Why didn't I think of that? I should have given them a calling card. Traveling on a budget isn't easy."

"He said you had the emergency number but I doubt you'll need it."

"I hope not," Julie agreed. "See you tonight."

❧

Why had she done that? She'd committed to spending another evening with Noah. Julie could only blame it on a moment of temporary insanity. Noah's sacrifices on behalf of her family entitled him to enjoyment of the holiday season. She couldn't refuse him that.

Just keep it casual, she told herself, catching Naomi's hood when a gust of wind blew it back. Julie glanced back to make sure the boys followed. They'd spent enough time outside today. She definitely didn't need them getting sick before Christmas.

Julie wasn't as confident as Noah was that she wouldn't need the emergency number, but she was determined to avoid using it if possible. At least Noah hadn't mentioned her losing Luke. Mari would have been on the next plane home.

She stayed busy that afternoon. Julie had never realized how much laundry a larger family generated. The housework, cooking, and laundry wore a body out, not to mention the children's constant demands.

By nightfall, Luke had been in time-out three times. No wonder Joey called him their challenge. At least she now knew she was capable of discipline. Julie looked forward to getting them fed and in bed for the night. She groaned when the doorbell rang and she remembered the tree decorating party.

"Mr. Noah's here," the boys chanted.

Julie opened the door. "Come in."

The boys ran at him and a mock tussle ensued.

"Enough," Julie called finally. "You boys get washed up. The pizza will be here soon."

After they left the room, Noah looked at her and said, "Don't tell me you're planning to put that monster on the van in here."

Julie shrugged. "What choice do I have? Matt cried and said his mom would let him have the tree."

Noah laughed. "Our buddy Matt pulled a fast one on you. Mari never asks for anything taller than seven feet. Actually, she said she had Mr. Simpson drop off a tree last year."

Julie released a heavy sigh. "It's going to be a long two weeks. I don't suppose you know where Joey keeps his saw?"

❧

Nothing was going the way she'd envisioned, Julie realized as she tucked Luke under the covers and kissed him good night.

The pizza party had been fun and then she and Noah had spent the next half hour wrestling the overgrown tree into the stand. Julie still wasn't too sure the tree that brushed the ceiling and took up an entire corner would remain standing on its own.

Her nephews liked the cartoon character lights but had demanded their decorations. Matt had led her to the ornament box in the hall closet. She wasn't surprised to find a variety of standard Sunday school issue ornaments.

"What is this?" she'd asked, pulling a foil-wrapped paper cup from the box.

"Don't you know a Christmas bell when you see one?" Noah asked when Julie twirled the bell by the string.

"Obviously not."

"That's mine, Auntie Julie," Matthew had said, taking it from her hand. "Let's put it right here in front."

"But, Matt, I bought all these great ornaments for the tree.

Don't you want to use them?"

"I like my bell."

"Okay." She'd reluctantly pushed aside the new items and they'd hung all the decorations in the box.

Tree decorating hadn't held the boys' interest for long and they'd charged around the room, falling over boxes. When Luke stepped into a box of ornaments, Julie yelled, "Stop running or you're all going to bed now!"

Noting her frustration, Noah had stepped in and said, "Hey, guys, want to show Aunt Julie what you're doing in the Christmas play?"

Though they'd pushed and shoved in the fight for the limelight, he'd quickly organized them.

Matt spoke his few words of dialogue and had constantly looked to Noah for prompting. Marc and Luke had non-speaking roles, though she couldn't imagine how they planned to keep the two of them still long enough to produce a play.

Now that the children had been bathed and were in bed, Julie and Noah sank into the living room chairs. She leaned back and stared at the evergreen gracing the corner of the room. "Did you notice anything about this tree?"

"You mean beyond its monstrous size?"

"Most of the ornaments are below the three-foot level."

"Little boy height," he said with a broad grin.

"Exactly." Julie pushed herself up out of the chair. "Oh well, I might as well finish decorating the green monster."

Noah stood and reached for the box of ornaments Julie had rescued from Luke's sneakered feet earlier. He used the ribbons she had tied on to hang them higher in the tree. "You were disappointed by the kids' reactions to your decorations."

He was too astute by far. "I'd hoped to please them. I should have known it wouldn't be easy. One thing I'll say about my nephews and niece is that they have minds of their own. And I'm proud they want to honor tradition even if I'm a bit disappointed I can't give them the perfect tree this year."

"Is perfection really that important?"

Julie held up the glass cartoon ornament for which she'd paid a hefty price. "I just thought the kids would love these."

"They do. But they like their ornaments, too. Don't you have ornaments that make it onto the tree every year no matter what theme you choose?"

Julie nodded, staring glumly at the tree. How different it was from what she'd planned. Noah had cut off a considerable amount just to get it into the house. Then finding a good side took some doing. At least the boys loved the musical lights, but she suspected she would hate them before the holidays were over.

"There are children in this world who have never seen cartoon lights. Some never see a Christmas tree. Above everything else, Joe and Mari's children know the true meaning of Christmas. The extraneous trappings can never be as important as the true gift of Jesus.

"Besides, this poor pitiful tree might never have had anyone to love it if you and the kids hadn't come along. You, with your big tender heart and great love for those boys."

"Good point. Even this tree deserves love. Let's just pray I can keep it standing through the holidays."

"So how was your second day with the kids?"

"Busy." Julie shifted ornaments higher up on the opposite side of the tree. "What about you? How's your sermon going? Joey told me you were looking forward to filling in for him."

"I do appreciate the opportunity to preach. Of course, Joe is a tough act to follow. The congregation at Cornerstone loves him a great deal. He preaches to a full house every Sunday."

"I'm sure you'll do well," Julie told him. "Lots of people come to church for Christmas services."

Noah smiled wryly. "I suppose I should be thankful for that, but I'd rather people came to hear the message God wants me to share with them."

She adjusted the drape of the light strand over the branches.

"They will. Give them time. You have years to serve God to your fullest."

"I'm ready now."

Julie turned to face him. "Then why follow Joey? Why not find a church of your own? A place where you don't have to live up to someone else's track record?"

"I need experience. Most churches consider me unproven material."

His response puzzled Julie. "Seems they wouldn't pass judgment until they'd heard you preach."

Noah picked up the tree topper, glanced at the tree and back at Julie. "You have those clippers handy? We need to shave off some branches if you plan to use this."

"I'll be right back."

When she returned with the clippers, Noah climbed up the stairs and pulled the treetop closer. After trimming up the branches and stuffing them in the garbage bag Julie provided, he slid the glass character into place.

"Can you trim this tree all the way down?"

Noah shook his head. "It would be easier to slip out tomorrow and get a new tree. Think the boys would notice?"

"Probably. So explain why you're unproven material."

"In your case, age has nothing to do with your ability. You're an up-and-coming computer whiz kid. When they consider my age, I lack maturity, and being single doesn't help."

"That's a plus about my job. No husband required."

"I've always been fascinated by your work. I wouldn't have a clue where to begin."

"Experience." Though she enjoyed her work as a software engineer, Julie rarely discussed it with noncomputer people. Her tendency to get technical often resulted in glazed expressions. "So you like the area?"

"Different accent. Hospitable people. Actually, it's a great place to live. I could see myself here for a while."

Julie fiddled with the ribbon she held, tying it into a bow.

Secretly, she admitted she liked the area, too. Back in the summer, Mari had insisted that she and Joe play tourist and Julie had enjoyed herself a great deal. They'd laughed as they crammed as much into one action-packed day as possible. They'd walked along the beach, played a game of miniature golf, and gone to the Pavilion amusement park. Then they'd stuffed themselves on fresh seafood and she'd begun to understand why so many people planned their vacations at the beach.

Still, she couldn't see herself living in Myrtle Beach. "I miss them all so much," Julie said. "I was heartbroken when the ministry called Joey and Mari away from Denver. I miss doing the aunt thing with the older kids and I barely know the twins."

Noah flashed Julie a sympathetic smile. "You and Joe grew closer after your parents died and now you live so far apart."

Her thoughts drifted back to the day Joey had called her friend's house to say her father was dead and her mother in the emergency room. Her dad had taken her mom for a drive in his pride and joy—the old MG he'd rebuilt. A deer had darted onto the highway, and in his effort to avoid it Joseph Dennis Sr. had rolled the car. The impact killed him. Her mother sustained a substantial amount of internal damage. Joey arrived minutes after the doctor pronounced Lillian Dennis dead.

At eleven, her parents' deaths destroyed her life. She'd always been their little princess and then they were gone. Julie had grieved a great deal for the loving parents who had been ripped from her.

Joey constantly reassured her that everything would be okay. The accident happened in May, just one week before the school year ended. Fear of the changes she'd have to make haunted Julie, but her twenty-four-year-old brother changed his life to make sure nothing changed for her.

He gave up his apartment and came home. Julie slept in her

bed, lived in the house she'd always lived in, and attended the school she'd always attended. She'd been fourteen when Joey and Mari married.

Once again, Julie had feared change, but Mari had loved and cared for her in the same way Joey had. Mari had worked with Joey, and when the time had come for Julie to go off to college, they'd helped with the costs.

"Yeah, Joey gave up everything for me."

"Seems so strange to hear you call him Joey."

"He tells me it's childish but he's always been Joey to me."

"What about me, Julie? Do you miss me, too?"

Before she could answer, Luke surprised them both when he joined them at the tree. He found the control switch that started music playing and then rubbed his eyes. "Nay-Nay's crying."

"Oh! I didn't hear her," Julie cried, thinking she should have added a baby monitor to the shopping list. "She and John aren't sleeping well. Probably missing their parents."

Noah swung the child into his arms. "Come on, buddy. I'll tuck you in while Aunt Julie takes care of your sister."

Julie took Naomi from the crib and changed her. Noah walked out of the boys' bedroom just as she stepped into the hall with the child.

"Can I hold her?"

Julie handed Naomi to Noah. "I'll get her milk."

Noah and Naomi were sitting in the rocker recliner when she returned. She passed him the cup and returned to hanging ornaments on the branches.

She glanced at Noah a few minutes later and found him studying the sleeping baby. "I can't get over how perfect they are," he admitted with a sheepish grin. "You'd better take her. I need to get out of here so you can get to bed."

"Thanks for your help, Noah."

"Thanks for the tree party. I enjoyed myself." He lifted his coat off the coatrack and slid it on. "Oh, don't forget the final play practice Saturday at four. We'll probably run through a couple of times since the play is Sunday night. There's a little party for the kids afterward."

"We'll be there. Are all the kids like Joey's? They seem a bit. . . um. . .reluctant."

"They'll do fine. Kids are born hams."

"Anything I can do to help?" Julie asked.

Noah winked. "Taking good care of my star performers is plenty."

four

After an early delivery the next day, Julie bundled the kids up and headed outside midmorning to work on the exterior decorations. The boys ran to play on the swing set as the twins watched from their stroller. She had brought all the boxes out onto the patio earlier to make things easier.

While people who lived in the area might consider it a cold day, Julie found it almost balmy in comparison to the December Colorado weather she'd lived with all her life. One of her friends had e-mailed her last night to tell her they had six inches of snow on the ground.

"What are you doing?" Noah asked.

Julie whirled to face him, clutching her chest. "Give a person a little warning next time."

"I saw you toting all these boxes and wondered what you were getting ready to do."

"Part of the shipment arrived today. My yard decorations."

"What sort of decorations?"

Was it her imagination or did he sound suspicious?

"I have tons of stuff," she said, stripping the tape from the box top to remove the inflatable cartoon character. "I can hardly wait for the kids to see it all lit up tonight!"

He grew silent and Julie glanced up at him. "Something wrong?"

Noah looked uncomfortable. "Hmm, Julie, this is the church parsonage. The congregation. . . Well, you know. . . Some of them might. . . What I'm trying to say. . ."

"Spit it out, Noah," Julie said impatiently. "You think the Cornerstone members won't appreciate the cartoon characters or outside lights on the church parsonage?"

He shrugged helplessly. "Some are concerned with appearances. They might find the decorations out of keeping with the true meaning of Christmas."

"Do they realize there are five kids in this house who are as entitled to rejoice as the next person?"

"Well, yes they do, but—"

"But nothing." Julie didn't bother to hide her exasperation. "The fact that their daddy is the minister and their home is the parsonage shouldn't prohibit them from having fun. And given the amount of money this church brings in from the day care, you'd think the membership could accept a few decorations for the kids. Tell me, if I drove by their homes, wouldn't I find similar yard decorations?"

"Probably. I just don't want repercussions for Joe when he comes back."

"He can handle them." Julie pulled the instruction sheet out of the box. "He said I could do whatever I wanted."

"Surely you realize he expects you to exercise restraint."

"So, I promise not to drain the electric company, but I do intend to string some lights and put up my decorations. If it makes you feel better, I have a Bethlehem Star for the porch and plan to put Joe and Mari's lighted nativity in the front yard."

"I'm sure that will be appreciated."

"So why don't you make yourself useful and help me figure this thing out?"

"Sorry, no can do," Noah said as he backed away. "That would make me an accomplice and I'm already in enough hot water as it is."

"Because of this?"

"No," Noah said. "A member took exception to the topic for the Sunday morning sermon."

"Didn't you say you planned to preach on loving your neighbor?" Noah nodded. "That's ridiculous. It's what Jesus says in the Bible, not the gospel according to Noah."

"These ladies have feuded for years. It never occurred to me that they would feel I directed the sermon at them. They weren't even on my mind."

"Joey says he tells them he's only a messenger for God."

"I doubt that would work for these ladies," Noah said. "And what do I tell the director of music? He accused me of trying to do his job when I named a couple of songs to go along with Sunday's sermon."

"Joey doesn't request specific music?"

"Not exactly. Rob pointed out that Joe recommends songs. I didn't think he would be offended."

"It's ridiculous that people get so out of sorts over little things. Particularly Christians."

"Sinners saved by grace, Julie. Christians are no different from everyone else. Our feelings get hurt, we feel insulted, and we get angry when injustices occur. And we seek repentance and try to do better."

"Whose side are you on anyway?"

Noah grinned at her. "I'm on the side of right. Joe is always advising me to proceed slowly and cautiously."

"This church needs to open itself to change."

"Churches are about balance, Julie. No one group can control the situation. Philippians 2:2 says, 'Make my joy complete by being like-minded, having the same love, being one in spirit and purpose.' I'd be remiss in my duties if I didn't ask forgiveness from those I've offended just as I've asked you not to go overboard."

Julie hated feeling controlled. Rebellion surged within her. "Consider me forewarned."

"They'll probably send me to talk to you later," Noah responded.

"The messenger for their dirty work, huh?"

"It would be my pleasure to visit with you and the kids."

Julie surrendered. "Okay, Noah, just for you, so you don't get in hot water with the congregation, I'll keep it as low-key as possible. I can put most of the kids' stuff in the backyard where they can see it from the kitchen and family room. I'd planned to anyway so the day care kids could see it from the playground."

"Thanks, Julie Joy."

"Anytime." She started to the house and whirled back toward Noah. "I do have a singing welcome Santa for the porch. You think I'd better put him in the foyer?"

"Probably best so he doesn't conflict with the nativity," Noah said, grinning when Julie made a face at him.

Julie recognized that her desire to defy Noah and decorate the yard as she pleased stemmed from her anger, but deep inside she knew he was right. Joey would have restrained her if he'd been there. It was so much harder to accept from Noah because she'd once considered him her soul mate. They'd shared so many fun times and now he seemed determined to control her.

By the time the inflated character rose to its ten-foot glory, lunchtime had arrived. Julie fought the temptation to stick the kids in the van and go for meals. Instead, she made toasted cheese sandwiches and soup.

Afterward, she cleaned the kitchen and put Naomi and John down for their naps. Matt and Marc went off to play and Luke wandered around the house in search of his favorite truck. When he couldn't find it, he came to her for help. They found it at the bottom of one of the toy baskets.

Julie pulled the box containing the singing welcome Santa into the living room. Once she removed all the wrappings, she found it was only two feet tall. Surely something held it in place. She settled on the sofa with the instructions and tried to figure out why her life-sized Santa was so short.

"What doing, Auntie Hulie?"

She looked up at Luke. "Reading instructions."

Luke leaned on the Santa's head and Julie heard it click. He cried out when the Santa sprang to its full height, knocking him backward. His weight must have released whatever held it in place.

Julie jumped to her feet and picked the child up. "Luke? Are you okay?"

Seeing the way he looked at the Santa before he walked out of the room, Julie doubted Luke would have much use for the decoration. Oh well, if she made Santa sing, maybe Luke would change his mind.

She reached for the instruction sheet again. After figuring out how to make Santa sing and placing him at the end of the staircase in the vestibule, Julie pulled the next box over and began assembling the reindeer. Somewhere there was a sleigh with a waving Santa to be unpacked.

Her thoughts returned to Noah. Day three and they'd eaten, decorated, and cared for the kids together, and yet she still felt so distant from him. She didn't want to need Noah Loughlin. He expected her to understand and accept her place in his life without question or regard to herself. Julie considered that selfish.

Maybe Noah believed he could gain experience here at Cornerstone, but Julie felt he could have done so closer to home. Closer to her. She couldn't help but feel he'd put distance between them on purpose. She suspected her age had motivated him to give her time. Whatever the case, she didn't plan to give him the opportunity to hurt her again. If he needed distance, he could have all he wanted.

The doorbell rang. As she passed within range of the motion detector, the Santa began to twist at the waist and sing. Julie smiled and opened the door. "Noah?"

"I'm on my lunch break. I thought I'd stop by and make sure everything's okay."

"You don't need to check on us so often," Julie told him, turning back toward the living room.

He followed her. "I wanted to make sure you understood about the decorating."

"I remember a time when you would have pitched in and helped. You're different."

"Not really. I still enjoy the things we did together, the time we spent with each other. Those are my fondest memories."

Memories. She'd become a fond memory. Not exactly where she wanted to be. The silence grew more awkward and Julie asked, "You want a sandwich?"

"I wouldn't mind."

"We had toasted cheese for lunch. I think there might be some ham if you prefer a hot ham and cheese."

"Sounds great."

He followed her into the kitchen and sat at the table when she refused his help. "I remember sharing more than one of these with you," he said when she handed him the plate.

"Quick and easy. What do you want to drink?" She listed his options and he chose milk.

He took a bite of the sandwich. "Tell me about Mac and Bo. How are they doing?"

Julie poured a glass of milk and pushed the refrigerator door closed. She set it on the table and shrugged. "I rarely see them. We're all busy."

"You're too busy for friends?" Noah asked.

"They were always more your friends than mine."

"They liked you, Julie."

"I liked them, too. It's a struggle to see everyone," Julie defended.

"You were in the same Sunday school class."

"Don't go there, Noah. We'll only argue."

He pushed the plate away, leaving half the sandwich uneaten. "Is there anything we can discuss without arguing? I'm trying to understand, Julie, but you're determined to make it more difficult every time I see you."

"So why don't you just stay away?" she snapped as she grabbed a cloth and wiped down the counter.

He stood and placed his hands on her shoulders, turning

her to face him. "Because I care about you."

Joey's words about Noah's popularity with the single women at Cornerstone came to mind. "I find that difficult to believe."

Anger changed his expression. "You know what, Julie? I don't think you care how I respond to that. You've already made up your mind. Believe what you want."

He stormed out of the kitchen and headed for the front door. Julie followed.

The Santa burst to life, directing Noah to have himself a Merry Christmas.

"Oh, shut up!" Noah yelled as he jerked the door closed.

five

The remainder of the decorations went up and the follow-up visit never occurred. Even though Julie resented not being able to go all-out for the kids, she accepted proving a point would only antagonize the membership, and she really didn't want to do that.

She'd opted for a religious theme in the front and hid the lights and cartoon characters in the backyard. It bothered Julie that people saw evil in innocence, but right now learning to be a temporary mother kept her fully occupied.

The main thing she'd already learned was nothing went as expected when you had five children. Just getting them up, fed, and dressed exhausted her but by no means diminished their incredible energy levels.

Julie spent her days running here and there, asking questions they couldn't answer, and searching the lists for guidance from Mari. She'd be lost without her sister-in-law's information.

On Wednesday she'd braved the mall to have the children's pictures taken with Santa. Marc took an intense dislike to the jolly one, and Julie talked him into posing by Santa's knee rather than sitting on his lap. All the framed photos sat on the fireplace mantel along with the children's stockings.

By Friday she'd become friends with the deliveryman who'd stopped by every morning to leave yet another box. With the last of the decorations in place, she'd been able to concentrate on her gift-wrapping after the children were in bed.

Today was the final play practice. "Matt, where is your costume?" she asked when she couldn't find the information anywhere.

He shrugged and said, "I don't know."

She breathed deeply and reminded herself he was only five. It didn't matter that he could name every cartoon character in the video they'd watched earlier. Things like costumes weren't as important. "You've got play practice this afternoon. Why don't we go over your lines?"

Matt continued to connect and stack plastic blocks as he recited his lines a couple of times. Julie had to prompt him both times and felt certain he wouldn't recall them Sunday night.

One of the many plans she'd carried through on before flying out of Denver was to purchase a video camera. She decided now would be a perfect time to videotape the boys and let them see their performances.

"Marc. Luke. Come here," she called.

Her breath stopped when both boys brushed past the tree as they raced into the room. "Don't run in the house," she instructed. "If I get my new video camera, will you guys show me what you do in the play?"

When Matt nodded, Marc and Luke did the same.

"I'll be right back." John stood on the sofa beside her. Julie grabbed him around the middle and rested him on her hip. He grinned at her and she asked, "Are you Aunt Julie's boy?"

"Me am!" Luke cried, racing after Julie and throwing his arms about her legs.

She caught herself just before falling against the wall. She'd never get used to the boy's ambushes. "Yes, you are," she agreed, patting him on the back. "Play with your brothers until I get back."

Julie had studied the operation manual during her flight and felt confident she could operate the camera—especially after her fellow passenger had recognized the video camera and shared some operating tips. She picked up the small black case and started downstairs.

She would leave the camera with Joey and Mari. Of course Joey would say no, but she'd already thought of a way around his refusal. After all, if he planned to raise her nephews and niece across the country, the least he could do was send her videos. Movies would be much better than pictures. And, he'd promised not to say anything about the expensive gifts. She'd see if he could keep his word.

She settled John on the sofa and placed the camera case at the opposite end. Removing the camera, she adjusted the viewfinder so she could see all the boys. John launched himself forward, eager to check out the new toy. Julie grabbed him just before he fell off the sofa and settled him in her lap. Filming while moving the busy fingers of a child intent on maneuvering the camera into his mouth took some doing. "Look, John," she said, indicating the viewfinder. "See your brothers?"

Onscreen, the boys jumped and shrieked, waving at the camera. The baby bounced up and down and responded in gibberish. Julie likened them to rubber balls, always on the go. Not that she was so old but watching them tired her out. John lunged for the camera again and Julie sighed. She felt guilty for wishing he'd taken a nap with Naomi, who slept in the playpen despite the turmoil in the room.

"We're going to make a movie to show Mommy and Daddy. Everybody's going to be in it. See, John wants to be a star," she said, struggling to pull the camera from the toddler's hold. "Who wants to talk first?"

"Me do!" Luke said, waving his arm as he jumped up and down. The entire room vibrated and Julie held her breath when the tree wobbled behind him.

"Luke, calm down. What did you want to say?"

He ran over to the tree and hit the switch that set the lights to flashing and songs to playing. "Moosic," he said, pointing to the tree as he started to dance.

Not to be outdone, Matt came over and pressed his face against the camera lens. "And I picked out the tree, didn't I, Auntie Julie?"

Julie stifled her laughter and agreed, "You sure did. Do you want to say something to Mommy and Daddy, Marc?"

He hung his head and remained silent, nearly breaking her heart when he began to cry.

Julie turned the camera off and laid it in the case as she placed John on the floor. She moved to where Marc stood and knelt beside him, wrapping the child in a hug. "What's wrong, sweetie?"

"I want Mommy and Daddy to come home."

"They'll be here soon and they'll tell you all about their special trip. I bet they bring you a great souvenir."

"What's a souvenir?" he asked with a tiny sniff.

"A special reminder of places we visit. Would you be my helper today?" she asked, hoping the camera would divert his attention from his missing parents.

When he nodded, Julie took his hand and led him over to the sofa. After settling John at her feet with a stuffed animal, she pulled Marc's tiny body closer and picked up the camera. "Look right here. Do you see Matt and Luke?"

He nodded.

"Okay, guys, are we ready?"

The phone rang, and Julie wished for a cordless phone or an answering machine. She made a mental note to provide either or both before she left for home as she placed the camera on the floor and ran to the kitchen.

"Hello, Julie."

"Noah. Hi."

"You sound out of breath. Playing with the kids?"

"Dashing for the phone."

"Sorry. I wanted to touch base and remind you about practice."

Except for a glimpse of him Wednesday night at church, she hadn't seen Noah since he'd stormed out of the house on Tuesday. He'd called a couple of times but remained suspiciously absent. Neither of them had brought up the argument. Maybe he'd decided he was better off without her. "I didn't forget. We're having rehearsal right now. I bought a video camera and we're making a tape for Joey and Mari. I think seeing themselves perform will help the boys."

He didn't respond.

"Don't you think it's a good idea? Noah?"

"How are they doing?"

"Matt and Luke are real characters. I don't think Marc is showbiz material."

"It's a church production. They'll do fine."

"A little extra rehearsal can't hurt."

"Don't push them, Julie. They're just kids. If they become overwhelmed, they won't do anything."

"Oh, come on, Noah."

"I'm serious. I know you mean well, but please don't *make* them practice. Do something fun instead. Make sure they eat lunch and get the little ones to take a nap. That helps more than all the rehearsals in the world. See you this afternoon."

"What does he know?" Julie asked aloud after replacing the receiver. He wasn't a parent, either. Besides, it was on the list. Item number 36—Go over Matt's lines with him. Mari had even written them in for her. And if that was what Mari wanted, that's what she'd get. No matter what Noah Loughlin said.

She returned to the living room to find Luke holding the camera upside down while Matt pretended to be a bear.

"Luke!" she yelled, grabbing the camera just before he let go. "This is not a toy, guys. If you want to look at it, ask. Otherwise, don't touch."

When Luke's lower lip wobbled at her stern words, Julie felt remorse. "Come here. You can help me and Marc film Matt showing your parents how he's turned into a bear." She sat on the floor next to John.

Matt started to growl and soon Luke abandoned her to join in. Marc decided he wanted to be in on the fun as well. Their antics were so funny that Julie burst into giggles. The harder she laughed, the worse they became, pushing each other away to stand before the camera. Luke cried out when Matt knocked him down. "Okay, guys, stop."

When she swiped tears from her eyes, John patted her face and said, "Cry?"

"It's okay, sweetie," Julie said, winking at the toddler. "Your brothers are funny bears. Matt, say your lines one more time and we'll watch the tape before lunch."

They weren't bored in the least, Julie thought as the jumble of little boys surrounding her on the sofa giggled at their own antics.

"You think your mom and dad are going to be surprised to find you've turned into wild animals?"

"Bears," Luke cried, growling again as he curled his fingers like claws.

The others followed suit.

"Let's make lunch." The boys followed her into the kitchen, and Julie soon had the meal on the table. So what if it was hot dogs and chips? They liked them. John nodded in his chair, jerking awake each time one of the boys shouted. Julie put him down for a nap and suggested Luke rest as well.

He crawled onto the sofa with the remote control. As he watched and rewound the tape repeatedly, Julie addressed Christmas cards.

When the grandfather clock gonged three o'clock, she put them away and said, "Luke, it's time to get ready for church."

"Don't want to."

"Well, you have to," Julie said, taking the remote and turning off the television. "They need you in the play."

"Don't want to," Luke repeated, jumping up and running from the room. She heard Joey's office door down the hall slam.

What do I do now? Julie wondered when five minutes passed with no sign of Luke. She couldn't help but speculate how

Joey and Mari dealt with their child's temperamental times.

She went to find the other kids, thinking she'd take care of Luke last. Julie soon had them ready to go, but Luke hadn't come out of hiding. She needed advice on this one. Perhaps Noah could give her some clues as to how Joey and Mari handled the situation. Julie dialed the church office. Soon Noah was on the line. "Does Luke have to practice today?"

"It's the final run-through before the performance tomorrow night."

"He doesn't want to."

"Because you rehearsed him?"

"What are you saying? That it's my fault?"

"It's not my fault, either," Noah said.

"I'm sorry but he said he doesn't want to," Julie stressed. "At least that's what he said when I turned the video off and told him it was time to go."

"What was he watching?"

"We made a video. He's watched it a couple of dozen times. How do Mari and Joey handle him when he's like this?"

"Can I speak to him?"

Julie pulled the long phone cord over to yell down the hall. "Luke, Pastor Noah wants to talk to you.

"At least he came out of the room," she told Noah when the door opened. She leaned against the counter and waited while Luke took the receiver and responded to Noah's comments with head nods.

"Answer him. He can't hear your head rattle."

He's consistent, Julie decided when the child said he didn't want to go three times in a row. Luke held the phone out to her and wandered off again.

"See what I mean?"

"Joe doesn't give in to Luke's stubborn streak. You shouldn't, either. Even if he's not in the play, you have to bring him. If nothing else, perhaps he'll see the others and decide he doesn't want to be left out."

He has a point there, Julie thought. "I'll stress that his parents will be very disappointed and see what happens."

"Hang in there, Julie," Noah urged. "Joe wouldn't allow him to drop out, either."

His encouragement helped. Joey was right. Noah had been a major help. Even when she resented his advice, Julie knew he was only trying to help. She hung up the phone and went to find Luke. Taking his hand, she said, "Come with me. I have something to show you."

In his parents' bedroom, Julie sat on the bed and pulled Luke into her lap. Picking up the list, she pointed to where his mother wrote about the play. "Don't you think your mom will be disappointed when she hears you didn't participate?"

He twisted against her, trying to get down. "Don't want to," Luke muttered again.

Julie restrained him and looked into his face. "Why?"

"Don't want to," he said again.

Noah had said Joey wouldn't let Luke win, but how had he emerged the victor in this battle of wills? She had no idea what had prompted the child to change his mind.

Julie released him. She returned the list to the nightstand and said, "Fine, but you have to go to church with us. You can't stay home alone. Get your coat."

With barely seconds to spare, Julie shepherded her charges across the churchyard. She didn't feel victorious in her dealings with Luke. The child had refused to leave the house until she'd located his favorite shirt. Since she had no idea which shirt that might be and Mari hadn't covered that information on the list, Julie had no idea what to do. Matt had saved the day when he pulled the bright blue knit shirt from the drawer.

Once inside the church, Julie guided Luke into the pew and held John and Naomi on her lap. She smiled at the woman who came over and introduced herself as Kimberly Elliott.

"I'm the church's drama queen," she said, waving her arms flamboyantly as she gave a little bow.

Julie laughed and snaked a hand over Naomi's head to shake hands. "I'm Julie Dennis. Pastor Dennis is my brother. I don't think we met when I was here this summer."

"I was on vacation." Kimberly touched both babies' cheeks and then spoke to Luke, who hid behind the pew. "Pastor Noah told me you weren't going to be in the play. Too bad," she said sadly. "You did a great job as the shepherd boy. Guess I'll have to find someone else for my surprise."

" 'Prize?'" Luke said, jumping up.

Kimberly nodded. "I have a real baby lamb. Guess I'd better find someone to take your place. Nice having you with us, Julie. Bye, kids."

Apparently, Luke didn't care for the idea of giving up his role when there were live props involved, and soon he was on his way to the front of the church. Julie breathed a sigh of relief. John wanted to walk the length of the pew, and when she tried to settle him down, he started to cry.

Noah came over to sit at the other end of the pew.

"I'm hopeless at this," she said when her efforts to calm the child failed.

Noah flashed Julie a reassuring smile as he picked John up. "You're doing a great job."

"I doubt Joey and Mari would think so. I've done nothing but feed them junk food—hot dogs and chips, burgers and fries, chicken tenders, cold cereal, pizza, and now they're getting away with murder because I can't discipline them. I even have a church play dropout." She didn't even want to think about having lost Luke at the store.

"They trust you with the kids. They know you love them and will see to it they're cared for properly."

Julie noticed the looks in their direction and felt terribly embarrassed. "I should take them home. Could you bring the boys home after practice?"

"I suppose," he said. "They're having a cast party afterward. I'd hoped you'd stick around for that."

Naomi started to cry. Helplessly, Julie looked from one crying child to the other.

"Why don't we walk with them a bit?" Noah suggested. "They get tired of sitting still."

"Don't you need to help out here?"

"They can spare me."

She followed him into the fellowship area. Noah put John on the floor and let him go, keeping watch on the toddler as he wandered across the big room. When Julie did the same for Naomi, the little girl followed her brother.

Volunteers worked busily setting up for the party. A huge tree stood on the corner of the stage area, all dressed in white.

"Beautiful tree," Julie said, aware of the wistfulness in her tone.

Noah picked up a couple of cups from the table and filled them with punch. "The church ladies made all the decorations. We're having a White Christmas celebration next Wednesday night. They've planned a variety of activities to appeal to all ages. I hope you'll come."

She flashed him a look of disbelief. "You think I'm brave enough to bring these kids to something like that?"

Noah grinned and nodded his head. "Sure. Chances are you'd be on your own before the evening begins. People here love the kids. By the way, you can put the babies in the nursery Sunday night."

"Oh good, I wanted to. . ." She stopped talking and ran over to release John's hold from the tablecloth he seemed determined to pull to the floor. She guided him back to where they sat. "I thought I'd tape the play for Joey and Mari."

"Actually, the church has a videographer."

Julie's attention perked up. "Really? I didn't know that."

"Cornerstone has an active music ministry. They also film Joey's sermons and deliver them to the homebound. There's been talk of a local television program but that hasn't gone anywhere."

"Joey never mentioned that."

"He'll do it if that's God's plan, but he's not eager to be on camera."

Her brother, the television star. She would have to razz Joey about that. Actually, she knew he had the charisma to be a television evangelist.

"Who's playing Santa for the Christmas party?"

"We don't do Santa at church," Noah said, waving at a teenage girl who entered through the side door. "I tell the Christmas story, instead."

"That's probably best. By the way, where are the costumes? Matt didn't have a clue."

"Here at the church. They use the same ones every year."

"I wish I could have been here earlier. A live nativity would have been fun for the kids," Julie said, her enthusiasm growing.

"You're doing it again," Noah said softly.

"What?" she asked curiously.

"Taking control of the situation. Julie, this congregation has done the same Christmas program for years. I imagine some of the grandparents probably did this play when they were children."

"Well, then it's long past time for a change."

"I hope you don't plan to rock the boat the entire time you're here."

. "Rock the boat?" she repeated, unable to control the mutinous frown on her face. "Well, blame it on whoever gave Joey the trip. If they hadn't sent my brother away, I wouldn't be here to interfere."

"You're not interfering," Noah said quickly. "You're a pastor's sister. You know about church politics."

"No, I don't do politics."

"This congregation does things the way their ancestors did them."

"Do the youth stay?"

"Joe said the congregation was primarily senior citizens when he arrived. Most of their children had moved their families on to more progressive churches."

No wonder they wanted Joey as pastor. He and Mari filled a pew, not to mention a Sunday school class. "That's exactly why they should be open to change. To make those kids want to grow up, marry, and raise their families in the church they've attended all their lives."

"The good news is those families are returning and others are joining. The number of children alone has increased tenfold since Joe took the job here."

Something else her brother hadn't told her. He'd never been one to toot his own horn, but Julie considered that quite an accomplishment.

"Joe gives full credit for that to the Lord," Noah told her. "He says all we can do is plant the seed and wait on God for the harvest. I look forward to having a church, to seeing how God uses me, but I have to accept that I'm just getting started in God's business."

"Isn't Joey's vacation your opportunity to shine?"

Noah reached down and lifted John onto his foot to give him a horsey ride. "Now isn't the time. Joe's worked hard here and I don't want him coming home to troubles I've caused."

She'd heard that one before. "But what about those people you told me about? The ones who are upset with you?"

"We're good. I explained that I didn't mean any harm and asked their forgiveness. Hopefully, Joe won't come home to a request for my resignation," he added with a smile.

"You think they would go that far?" Julie asked, horrified.

"No," he said quickly. "My job is secure."

Julie couldn't help but wonder what Noah would do if his job were terminated. Would he return to Denver? Or would he go elsewhere? She restrained her curiosity and changed the subject. "I've been trying to come up with something for the kids on Christmas Eve. What do you think about Santa dropping off my gifts to them?"

"It might be a little confusing. Santa coming on Christmas Eve and again on Christmas morning."

He had a point. "I thought about having a birthday party for Jesus at the house on Christmas Eve."

Noah studied her for a few moments. "You're always thinking, aren't you?"

"I just want things to be special for them this year."

"So they don't forget Aunt Julie?"

A frown pinched her forehead. "You're really down on me today. I don't want them sad over the Christmas holidays because they miss their parents."

One of the ladies asked if it was okay to give Naomi a cookie. Julie said yes. John laughed as Noah swung him on his foot.

"They don't look particularly depressed to me."

"You wouldn't understand."

"Try me," he challenged.

Julie didn't say anything for several seconds and then the truth poured out of her. "Joey gave up a lot for me over the years. I owe him, and he's never let me do anything to repay him. I can't fail on this one little thing he's asked of me."

"Did it occur to you that Joey did what God led him to do? He loves you, Julie, and his joy comes in seeing you grow in God and prosper."

"Still, I could have done more over the years. Like this trip, I didn't know they wanted to visit the Holy Land. I wish he'd let me do something without having to force it down his throat."

"Looks like he did. Don't you think these two weeks mean more to Joe than any monetary gift you've ever given them? Your willingness to give up your time this summer and again, now, proves your love beyond measure."

His comment shocked Julie. Taking time off for her family seemed more of a gift for her. "I never considered it as anything more than being there for the family I love."

Like a strike from a bolt of lightning from above, Julie realized that same sense of love had driven Joey to care for her after their parents' deaths.

Noah set his foot on the floor and offered a hand to help John stand. "It's not wrong to want people you love to have nice things and it's great that you can provide them, but even if you were broke and sleeping on their couch, Joe and Mari would love you."

John toddled off to play peekaboo with one of the adults. Noah appeared amused when Naomi came over and plopped down on his foot. He grabbed her hands and lifted her into the air. "Why don't you just go with the flow and stop trying to organize? These little guys don't know the meaning of the word. Enjoy spending time with the kids. Give them the gift of yourself."

Julie sensed an underlying reason for Noah's direction. "What experience taught you that?"

"It's obvious, huh?" When she nodded, he said, "I have a brother with type A personality. He has a wife, two children, and all the plans in the world. Toby nearly worked himself to death until he got the wake-up call a couple of years ago."

Julie shook her head. She smiled when Naomi mimicked her action. "I'm not like that. I just like organization."

Noah's knowing look disputed her claim. "Just so long as you aren't into denial."

"Very funny. I know my limitations."

"I'm not convinced."

One of the women stepped from the kitchen and called that practice would be over in five minutes.

Noah set Naomi on her feet and stood. "Time for announcements. You coming?"

She sighed. "The twins won't sit still. I'll stay here with them."

"I'll be happy to keep an eye on them for you, Miss Dennis."

The volunteer was the young woman who'd entered the fellowship hall a few minutes before. Dubious, Julie looked at the teenager. She was barely sixteen.

"Good idea, Robin," Noah said, grabbing Julie's hand. "Don't worry. She babysits often for Joe and Mari."

"Okay, just long enough to hear the announcements," Julie told the girl as Noah dragged her from the room. "I'll be right back."

"Take your time. I won't let them out of my sight."

"I really shouldn't take advantage of her like that," Julie said as Noah rushed her to the sanctuary. "She's helping prepare for the party."

"We'll be back before you can say all five kids' full names ten times," Noah said with a laugh.

six

After announcements, the cast members poured into the fellowship hall. Making sure her brood stayed out of trouble kept Julie busy. The volunteers had organized games and food. The masterpiece of the dessert table was the cake decorated to resemble a nativity.

"Who did that?" she asked Noah.

He studied it for a few minutes. "I'd say Natalie Porter. Avery will be upset."

"Why?" she whispered.

"They have a standing rivalry. Avery owns the bakery and Natalie makes specialty cakes in her home."

"So why didn't he make one, too?"

Noah shrugged. "Probably no one asked him. He doesn't have her flair for the original. You should get a slice of that cake. What Natalie does with cakes could be a sin."

Noah was right about the children. Matt, Marc, and Luke sat with families of their friends. One of Robin's friends had joined her and they begged to watch the twins.

"Okay, but come and get me the moment they get to be too much. I thought you were joking when you said I'd be alone," Julie told Noah.

"Mari never hesitates when anyone expresses an interest in spending time with the kids."

Maybe that's how she keeps sane, Julie thought.

After going through the line, they joined Kimberly Elliott at her table.

"How did practice go?" Julie asked as Noah held her chair for her.

"The lamb jumped out of Luke's arms," Kimberly said with

73

a laugh. "They were all chasing the poor thing. It took another ten minutes to get them going again after that. I'm glad Luke decided to participate."

"He couldn't refuse. You had him from the moment you said there was a baby lamb."

"Quite possibly the most stupid thing I've ever done," Kimberly said. "I may have to tie it to Luke tomorrow night so it can't run away."

They all laughed.

"Excuse me, ladies," Noah said. "I'll be right back.

"I told Noah the kids would enjoy a full live nativity."

"I wish," Kimberly said softly and then looked embarrassed. "He told me the play never changes."

The woman nodded, lowering her voice as she spoke. "I'd so love to produce different dramas for Christmas and Easter, but I don't think the idea would go over well."

"You won't know if you don't try," Julie said.

The woman appeared thoughtful. "I've been working on an Easter play for some time now. Maybe I'll approach Pastor Dennis when he gets home and ask his opinion."

"Do that. I'm certain Joey would be open to the idea." Julie dug her fork into the dessert. "Noah said this cake could be a sin," she said, taking another bite.

"Isn't it, though? Natalie makes excellent cakes."

Noah sat down. "What are you ladies talking about?"

"Julie thinks I should ask Pastor Dennis about the play I've written for Easter," Kimberly said.

Noah glanced at Julie.

"You think it's a bad idea?" Kimberly asked hesitantly.

"Not at all," he said with an easy smile. "I had no idea you'd written a program."

"I've written lots of stuff. Even have some Christmas and Easter programs published."

"I'm impressed. You've been hiding your light under a bushel."

Kimberly flashed him a shy smile. "It's my hope to one day see one of the programs at Cornerstone."

"Then by all means, ask Pastor Dennis for guidance," Noah said. "I'd love to see your production. I'm sure the congregation will be impressed to hear we have an author in our congregation."

Kimberly glanced at her watch. "It's five thirty."

"Guess that's my cue to get ready," he said, winking at them before he headed to the office.

"Noah is a nice guy," Kimberly said, her gaze following him across the room. "Mari mentioned that you and he dated. You make a nice couple."

Were they a couple? Once she'd gotten past her resentment, it had been easy to slip back into the idea of a relationship. But in a few days she'd return home and he'd stay here. Julie couldn't help but wonder if Kimberly's interest was more than passing curiosity.

Noah reappeared dressed as Simeon. The kids giggled when their youthful assistant minister emerged as an elderly man. He took a seat on the stage and called to the children to gather round him on the floor. Instead of the usual spiel about good boys and girls, he launched into the story of the first Christmas. Julie found it refreshing that Cornerstone didn't celebrate the commercial aspect of the holiday.

That's what I forgot, Julie thought. Buying gifts for the kids would not demonstrate the most important part of the Christmas experience. She had seen an angel tree at the mall. Maybe they could pick out a name and buy gifts for needy kids.

After Noah passed out bags of goodies to the kids, he left the stage and came to stand by her side. "So how did I do?"

"Great," she said, glancing down at Luke and Marc to find them busily dumping their bags onto the floor. She knelt to pick up the stuff. "Wait until we get home."

"Mine," Luke said when she inadvertently put his gift into Marc's bag.

One of the mothers approached and spoke to the boys. She reached out to shake Julie's hand. "Hello, Miss Dennis. I'm Merline Jenkins. I thought perhaps Matt could come over one day next week and play with my Jeremy."

What should I do? Julie wondered. She glanced over her shoulder at Noah.

"Mari and Merline often trade off play dates," he said.

Julie wondered if she could talk the woman into taking all the boys for a few hours. "I'll check the schedule and let you know what date is good."

"Wonderful. Maybe having someone to play with will take Jeremy's mind off Christmas. He keeps asking how many more days."

"I wouldn't be so sure of that," Julie said. "Matt's just as excited."

When they started getting the kids into their jackets, Noah asked, "Can I walk you home?"

"If you want." Julie zipped John's coat closed and handed him to Noah before picking up Naomi off the makeshift bed. She wrapped the sleeping child's coat about her and said, "Come on, guys. Time to go."

At the house, Noah unlocked the door and they moved into the living room. The boys flung coats right and left, while John came to Noah for assistance. Julie laid Naomi on the sofa by her side. John toddled over to the toy box.

Noah settled back in the armchair. "I see the tree is still standing."

His words reminded Julie of her plan to secure it to the wall. Luke had almost knocked it over earlier in the day while playing with the switch that activated the lights. She closed her eyes and held her breath every time the boys raced about the room. She really needed to find some string. "Don't breathe hard or it'll fall," Julie cautioned.

As if to prove her point, Marc ran into the room and sent it to rocking. "Luke's a bad boy, Auntie Julie."

Though there were times Julie felt hard pressed not to agree with him, she said, "Don't be a tattletale, Marc. Go play."

When the child ran out, Noah laughed and said, "Seems to be holding up well to me."

"It's a Christmas miracle."

They laughed again.

"That was nice of Mrs. Jenkins to invite Matt over. Of course I don't know how Mari stands adding another child to the group on a regular basis."

"Mari takes it all in stride. She's a great mom."

Julie agreed wholeheartedly. "I'm tempted to offer Mrs. Jenkins all three of the older boys," she said. "I need to finish my shopping but don't dare take them with me after what happened last time."

"Take them to the church day care."

Somehow it didn't seem right to burden others with her responsibilities. "I couldn't."

"Come on, Julie," Noah encouraged. "Give yourself a break."

"Maybe for a couple of hours," Julie relented. "I never realized how hard being a mother is."

"It's harder when you jump into a ready-made family," Noah said. "Having babies one at a time lets you ease into the situation and gain experience as you go."

"You inspired an idea today."

Noah groaned. "Figures. I tell you to take a break and you're inspired to do something else."

"No, it was your Christmas story. I got to thinking about how I've shown the kids a materialistic side of Christmas and thought maybe I'd take them all to the angel tree in the mall and let them choose a name and help me buy the presents. What do you think?"

Noah appeared to give the matter some thought. "How would you explain Santa not coming to those kids' homes?"

"I hadn't thought that far ahead. I suppose it might be confusing for them to grasp the concept. I could tell them

Santa picks the stuff up at the mall."

"And put the elves out of business?" he teased.

"Okay, what if I say we're buying special gifts for special kids?"

"Too special for Santa?" He shook his head. "Joe often talks to them about kids who don't have as much as they do. He wants the kids to understand Christmas is about Jesus' birth. They could put money into the Salvation Army buckets."

"What about church families? Anyone need anything?"

"The congregation looks out for them. This side of you fascinates me."

"What do you mean?" Julie asked, puzzled by his comment.

"Your need to give."

"Even if I don't get to church as often as I should, I do thank God for the blessings He gives me daily. I know my successes belong to Him. I just don't have time to get out there and do all I'd like to do."

"I'll keep my ears open just in case. People come into the church office fairly regularly this time of year."

A couple of minutes passed before Noah said, "I need to apologize. I behaved badly Tuesday. Apparently I haven't made my intentions clear."

"I wasn't making accusations, Noah. I can certainly understand that we weren't in the same place in our relationship. It's only natural that you'd want to find a spirit-filled woman to help with your ministry. Kimberly Elliott is very nice."

Bewildered, Noah exclaimed, "I'm not looking for another woman!"

"Then why would Joey say you're popular with the women here at Cornerstone?"

"I don't know. Maybe he was teasing you."

Something clicked in her head. "Or trying to make me jealous?"

"I doubt that. Joe didn't realize how serious I was about you until I told him."

"Noah, what did you do?" Julie asked suspiciously.

"He sort of asked my intentions."

Just what she needed—her overprotective brother involved in her romantic relationship. "What did you say?" she demanded, not bothering to disguise her exasperation.

"That I felt you were avoiding me."

Julie squirmed uncomfortably. Noah wasn't wrong there. She hadn't wanted to talk with him until she got her emotions under control for fear she'd tell him exactly how she felt. Now he seemed determined to bring their problems to the surface.

"This is between us, Noah. And Joey did tell me the women really liked you." She felt herself losing control. Julie didn't want to have this conversation—not now, not ever.

His scowl threw her off guard. "What are you talking about? Can't I talk with another woman without being seriously interested in her? Joe does it all the time. I don't see Mari getting all out of sorts."

"Because Mari is more secure in her place in Joey's life," Julie said pointedly.

"You feel insecure about me? I thought you knew how much I cared."

"I'm not a mind reader."

Noah's mouth dropped open. "I showed you all the time."

"You treated me like a casual date, Noah Loughlin. If we'd been serious, you would have consulted me before making your final decision. We would have discussed the options rather than you driving off to South Carolina without looking back."

"I did this for us. You resent the decision I made?" When she hesitated, he said, "Tell me, Julie."

"When you announced you were coming to Cornerstone, I felt like I didn't matter. I hate it when Joey treats me like a child, and I liked it even less when you did the same."

"I didn't." His helpless little boy look didn't help.

Julie struggled to keep her irritation under control. "Be

honest, Noah. You believed I was too young and felt you could go off, gain experience, and come back to pick up where we left off. You expected me to wait for you but didn't bother to ask if I would."

"You are young."

"You're only four years older than me. What makes you so much wiser?"

Noah looked more surprised with every revelation.

"Obviously nothing from your viewpoint. I never intended to pick up where we left off. If you'd noticed from all my efforts, I've been trying to keep our relationship going."

Julie did a one-handed sweep through her hair, moving it out of her face. "You certainly have a different idea of what that involves than I do."

"Okay, let's discuss this after the fact. How would you have expected me to deal with my options?"

His efforts to make her see reason frustrated Julie. "Will you watch the twins while I check on the boys?"

Noah agreed and she ran upstairs. The older boys played in their room. Luke drove his truck along the upstairs hallway.

She returned downstairs to find Naomi had awakened from her nap and joined John on the floor. The party food had filled Julie, but she knew the babies were probably ready to eat.

Noah followed her into the kitchen. "Are you going to answer me?"

"The twins need dinner and I need coffee."

After filling the twins' sippy cups, Julie started a fresh pot of coffee. Noah sat at the kitchen table after asking if he could help. She took toddler food from the cabinet and prepared plates for the twins. Then she took the cake plate Maggie had brought over yesterday and slid it onto the table.

"You should have told me," Julie said as she handed him a small plate, "then asked my opinion on the matter. We could have listed pros and cons and determined whether it was the most advantageous option."

Noah eyed her curiously. "You don't see the value of me working here at Cornerstone with Joe?"

Julie served herself a piece of cake and took a bite before sipping her coffee. "Not particularly. You're standing in his shadow. Not forming your own."

"I wasn't ready to pastor a church. Look at the mistakes I've made here this week."

"Trial and error, Noah. That's how we determine what works."

"In your field maybe. Churches have long-standing traditions that can't be discounted because I think my ideas work better."

"Sounds restrictive to me."

"But necessary for a cohesive church. There are enough destructive elements at work already without a pastor tearing his congregation apart. You're a free thinker, Julie. I admire that about you, but I have to be more methodical. I sought God's guidance in my decision."

"It's too late to change the situation now."

"Tell me what you want me to do, Julie."

"Does it really matter? You'd still have to seek God's guidance, and since He led you here in the first place, I hardly think He's going to send you home to Denver. You start praying about a transfer and you could end up in Alaska."

Noah's lips curved at Julie's musing. "Have you ever considered living in Alaska?"

"No, and I don't plan to, either."

"You need to open your mind to the possibilities, Julie Joy. God can use you anywhere in the world."

"Or He can leave me exactly where I am."

"Has it occurred to you that He's led you here twice in six months?"

"Well, yes, but not to stay."

"And yet you've spent at least two weeks both times."

"What's your point, Noah?"

He cupped the mug in his palms and met her gaze with one of determination. "I was wrong not to discuss this move with you. You're partly right in assuming I struggled with your age—but only because I don't want to rush you. I've been praying about us, Julie. Seeking God's guidance as to whether you're the one He intends for me. I know now that you are and I don't want to lose you. Please don't let distance become the barrier that destroys us. We can make it work. I know we can."

"You'd better tell me how. I don't share your vision."

The twins protested their restriction in the high chairs. Julie released them and set them on their feet. They toddled toward the living room and she followed.

"What if the promotion opportunity had been yours?" Noah asked as he followed on her heels. "What would you have done?"

She whirled around. "I would have told you and asked your opinion. That much I do know."

Noah's look was one of remorse. "I've enjoyed spending time with you these past few days, Julie. I miss you far more than you know, but I understand your anger. I admit, my failure to seek your opinion doesn't exactly support my statement that I have serious feelings for you. What can I do to convince you?"

Julie couldn't begin to explain how abandoned she'd felt after he'd left. How afraid. What could she do? Pick up where they left off and accept long-distance calls for a relationship until God led Noah to take another church? Who knew where he'd end up in the future? "I believe you realize you hurt me with your actions, but we still have a problem."

The conversation trailed off with the boys' arrival. Matt and Luke crawled up on the chair arms on each side of Noah, while Marc chose to join John on the floor.

Julie's gaze moved from person to person. How like a family they seemed, the two little boys in earnest conversation with Noah, and Marc, Naomi, and John playing at their feet. The homey warmth of the room contributed to the illusion. Mari and Joey might not have the most expensive furnishings in the world, but they had a nice home—a home that never lacked in love.

At Luke's request, Julie popped in the boys' video for Noah. He laughed heartily at their antics.

"You guys really know how to put on a show," he told them a few minutes later when he reached for his jacket. "I need to get home and put the final touches on my sermon."

Julie walked him to the door. "Are you nervous?"

"A little. It's in God's hands. You are going to be there, aren't you?"

"I told Joey I'd take the kids to church."

He kissed her cheek. "See you in the morning. Say a prayer for me."

"I will."

Noah paused and grasped her hands tightly in his. "I need to make you a promise, Julie Joy. If you forgive me, I'll never make another life-altering decision without consulting you first. I never left you behind. I've kept you in my heart. And I did look back." He squeezed her hands one last time and released them. "I am serious about my intentions. Meanwhile, we both need to seek God's guidance for our lives."

Later, Julie knelt by the bed to honor Noah's request. She prayed his sermon would reach the people God intended.

Unknowingly, he had stirred her to thinking of how she had pushed God lower on her list. She prayed for forgiveness, vowing to do better in the future. Concluding the prayer with an earnest request for God's continued guidance concerning her and Noah's relationship, she climbed beneath the covers.

As she lay there considering the revelations of the conversation, Julie thought about how communication breakdowns destroyed so many relationships. She didn't want to be a statistic, but she honestly didn't know any way to resolve their problem. Noah might be willing to wait, but she was ready to move on with her future. She loved him but she couldn't share the truth with Noah yet. Telling him of her love would only make her more vulnerable.

seven

The following morning, Julie scrambled out of bed late, confronted with the chore of getting the children fed, dressed, and to church on time. *Joey would never forgive me if they missed church on my first Sunday,* Julie thought as she rushed to shower.

Nothing was where it should be and with five minutes to go, they scrambled around in search of Naomi's patent leather shoes. At least Joey and Mari would be around next Sunday to help.

As organized as her sister-in-law was, she probably laid everything out the night before. Julie should have checked, but come to think of it, she hadn't seen the list since the day before when she and Luke had been dealing with the play situation.

"Auntie Julie, hurry!" Matt screamed.

She ran to the bathroom to find the toilet overflowing. Julie jerked clean towels off the racks and spread them about to catch the water. "What caused this?"

Matt shrugged and shook his head. Marc looked like he had something to say. "Marc?"

"Luke's a bad boy."

"Not!" Luke said, shoving Marc.

"Are, too!" Marc yelled, pushing back. Luke fell on the tile floor and started to cry.

"Boys, stop." Julie picked Luke up and made sure he hadn't fallen in the water. She held their shoulders to keep them apart. "Why is Luke bad?"

"He put Nay-Nay's shoe down there."

Julie groaned when Marc pointed to the toilet bowl. All eyes focused on Luke. The boy dropped his head.

Facing the monumental question of how to handle this, Julie simply didn't know what to do. She knew his parents would not allow Luke to escape punishment. But right now she knew dealing with the emergency was more important. Maybe Mari had listed a plumber's name.

She stepped into the bedroom and came right back to ask, "Have any of you seen the papers your mommy left for me?"

Marc nodded and pointed to the toilet.

"Luke, you didn't!" Julie cried, fighting the strong urge to spank the child. "Why?"

"Mommy said I had to go pway."

"Was this what you were trying to tell me last night, Marc?"

The child nodded. Tears welled up in her eyes as Julie prayed for patience. Why hadn't she listened to Marc when he'd tried to tell her about Luke's behavior?

She felt like she was in a rowboat left adrift in the middle of the ocean without oars. Every fact she needed to survive the next week was gone. Literally, down the toilet.

"What you did was wrong, Luke," Julie told him sternly. "You've destroyed important items that didn't belong to you and you've caused a problem with the house."

Glancing around to make sure the water had stopped, Julie decided to take the older kids to church and come back to clean up the mess.

After getting the boys to the right Sunday school classrooms, she started back down the stairs, carrying John and a shoeless Naomi in her arms.

"You're not staying?"

Julie turned to find Noah standing in the hallway outside the church office. Her breath caught in her throat at the sight of him in his navy suit.

She'd been looking forward to hearing him preach. Julie very much wanted to hear his message for the congregation.

"Oh, Noah, I'm in big trouble. Luke flushed Mari's list down the toilet."

Noah started. "You're kidding. Why would he do that? When?"

"Remember last night when Marc told me Luke was a bad boy?" Noah nodded. "Guess he figured if there's no list, he wouldn't have to do anything. I needed that information to prepare for Christmas Day. I'm totally out of my element here. That list had the menu, the whereabouts of the kids' Christmas presents, even the people Mari and Joe wanted to invite to dinner. He flushed Naomi's shoe, too."

"What did her shoe do to him?"

"Who knows? He probably tripped over it or something. There's water all over the bathroom floor. I have to call a plumber and no idea who to contact."

"The church's plumber is also a member," Noah said as he walked over to where she stood. "I'm sure he'll take care of the situation this afternoon."

"Well, that takes care of the toilet, but what about the list?" she asked, tears trailing down her face.

Noah thumbed them away and took John in his arms. "Stop now or you'll have them crying, too. The list is gone, Julie. You'll do the best you can. You can handle this with God's help. You know you can."

Julie felt her heartbeat quicken. Noah ministered because he cared for people, because of his ability to comfort, reassure, and help them believe everything would be okay if they just trusted God.

"Let's put the babies in the nursery. We'll check the house and then come back for services."

"You're not dressed for plumbing problems and Naomi doesn't have any shoes," she protested.

"I don't plan to make the repair, Julie. Just turn the water off. And haven't you noticed that Naomi spends most of her time barefoot? Luke probably figured she didn't need shoes, anyway."

❧

Julie slipped into the pew with Matt, Marc, and Luke just

moments before the choir began to sing. She'd never been so exhausted. Getting herself out of the house every morning was challenge enough, but adding five small people and a bathroom disaster to the mix almost made it a near impossibility. It had taken a great deal of effort, but the children were in church. A smile tugged at her mouth. Joey would be proud.

She'd tossed the wet towels into the bathtub after determining the water had stopped. The doorbell rang and Noah had opened the door to Robin's friend, who had come in search of Julie. Evidently, Luke had been overcome by remorse and had cried for Auntie Hulie until they'd located her.

Moments later, they stood in the hallway outside his classroom. His sobs and "I torry, Auntie Hulie" tugged at Julie's heart. She held him close and whispered about destroying other people's possessions.

Once he'd calmed down, she took him back into the classroom. Julie had watched the kids shower their teacher with Christmas gifts, embarrassed that she hadn't thought to buy gifts for the children's teachers. Of course, Mari could have had that on the list. She'd never know.

After their Sunday school lesson, they'd worked on a craft project. When Julie offered to help, Natalie Porter had quickly accepted.

"I don't mind the lessons but I don't like crafts at all."

Surprised, Julie had exclaimed, "Really? After that cake you made for the cast party, I figured you'd try anything. I've never seen anything so incredible."

Natalie grinned as she continued to place red pipe cleaners on the table. "Thanks. Too bad the kids can't craft with cake decorations. We could really make progress if that were the case."

"That reminds me. I'd love to order a couple of cakes for Christmas. Are you booked up?"

"Pretty much. I promised Mari two cakes already. Do you think you'll need more?"

Julie shook her head. "I didn't realize she'd ordered them. Luke flushed my lifeline down the toilet last night. Mari had listed everything for me. Now it's gone."

Natalie glanced at Luke and back at her. "What will you do?"

Julie shrugged. "The best I can."

"Let me know if I can help," Natalie said as she assisted a child with glue.

Julie appreciated the woman's offer. "You can join us for dinner if you don't have other plans."

"I have friends coming down for the holiday. Thanks for asking, though."

"Bring them along."

"I'll let you know," Natalie had promised.

Emulating the adults around them, the boys pulled hymnals from the back of the pew. Julie smiled when Luke held his upside down and sang the traditional Christmas hymn along with the choir. When the song ended, all three boys sat and laid the books on the seat beside them. No doubt they understood bad behavior would not be tolerated in the sanctuary.

The choir sang and then there was another congregational song. The music director announced a solo and then young Robin moved to the microphone. Her solo about the gift God gave His people at Christmas moved Julie to tears.

Noah rose and stepped to the pulpit. "If you would open your Bibles to the book of James, chapter 1, verse 17 and read with me. 'Every good gift and every perfect gift is from above, coming down from the Father of the heavenly lights, who does not change like shifting shadows.'

"The holiday season is upon us. A time for visiting with family and friends. Hustle, bustle, and good cheer. Shopping, decorating homes, writing cards, planning dinners, and making far more plans than we think we'll ever complete. A time for worries about whether our gifts will be liked, whether we've forgotten to buy a gift, or just simply because we have no idea what to buy. I see some of you agreeing with me.

"All those things are activities of the season, not reasons. There's only one real reason we celebrate Christmas and that's the birth of Jesus Christ. Listen to this scripture again."

Noah reread the verse, emphasizing the words to make his point. "There's *only one true, perfect gift* and *that's Jesus Christ.* Those who know Him as their Savior know exactly what I mean. Those who don't, continue to search for the missing element in their lives. The reason for their unhappiness, their discontent, their unease."

Julie glanced over her shoulder to see how people were responding to Noah. They appeared to be listening, nodding with every point he made. Noah danced on her toes with every word he spoke. She had busied herself with activities almost to the point that she'd opted to skip services this morning.

"How easy is it to know the Lord as your Savior? It requires a decision. A willingness to say 'I am a sinner.' A willingness to repent of those sins. A willingness to throw out the old and accept the new. A willingness to accept the gift of love.

"In a few days some of you will make resolutions for the New Year. The one life-changing resolution anyone can make is to commit his or her life to God.

" 'That's too easy,' you say," Noah said, stepping around the pulpit to the open stage area. " 'I'd never keep such a resolution.'

"It's not a commitment you make and then forget about in mid-January when the other resolutions fall by the wayside. It's a vow of change. A vow to do away with the old. To become new again. Reborn.

"If you're searching for the perfect gift for yourself, the 'one size fits all, never has to be returned, perfect gift,' choose salvation.

"Choose a Friend who walks with you even when you're alone. A Friend who never forsakes you. Brothers and sisters in Christ who welcome you into the fold with love.

"Do this and once you take that meaningful step, I promise that you'll never be sorry you did."

The service proceeded to the conclusion and an announcement about the children's play that night. During the closing prayer, Noah moved to the door to greet people as they left.

She and the boys picked up the twins from the nursery then walked across the yard to the house. As she changed the twins into play clothes, Julie considered the day as better for having attended Sunday services. Noah's sermon had been right on target. God had given the only true gift.

A few minutes later, Noah brought the plumber over. The older boys watched as the man removed the shoe, but the papers were gone. Julie suspected his stern warning about "things that don't belong in the toilet"—which he'd diplomatically directed toward her—had impacted Luke more than anything she might say on the subject ever would.

When the plumber left, Julie invited Noah to join them for lunch. He'd sat in Joey's chair and entertained the kids while she prepared and served the meal. Afterward, he'd helped clear the table and told her he had to run over to the hospital to visit a church member. "I'll see all of you at church tonight."

"Thanks, Noah."

He'd kissed her cheek and whispered, "Don't look so blue, Julie. God will provide."

After he had gone, Julie touched her cheek and prayed that God would indeed show her the way.

eight

After she tucked the children in for a nap, Julie lay on her bed, struggling to recall the bits and pieces of Mari's list that she had read. Why hadn't she put it in a safer place? Probably because it had survived the week before Luke decided to destroy his mother's missive.

Tomorrow she'd start working on the menu. She felt certain Mari's list involved lots of cooking but opted to simplify. Julie decided to order a few items to make the day easier for all concerned. Mari wouldn't feel like cooking after the long flight home.

Julie had barely caught her breath before the boys had to be back at church Sunday evening. The twins toddled off to play when Julie put them down in the church nursery.

"Too bad you have to miss the play," she told Maggie.

"I won't." She pointed to the television monitor on the wall.

"With all these babies?"

"I see enough to know what's going on. Sometimes they're so taken by something on the screen that they actually stop to watch."

"Thanks for taking care of Naomi and John."

"It's my pleasure."

Julie came back up the hallway to find everyone busy getting the children into costume. "Can I help?"

Kimberly shoved a hanger into her hand. "Help Matt into this and start praying none of them forget their parts," she added with a broad smile. "It's in God's hands now."

Julie settled into the front row seat beside Noah a couple of minutes before showtime.

"Everything under control?" he asked, taking her hand in

his and giving it a gentle squeeze.

She nodded. Someone had been busy since this morning; the stage sets had turned Cornerstone Church into Bethlehem. She could almost imagine herself there. "Joey and Mari didn't have to travel to see the Holy Land," she whispered.

"It is impressive. Kimberly doesn't do anything halfway."

Julie glanced at him. "You like her, don't you?"

"As a sister in Christ."

"I like Kimberly. She's a fun person. Shh," she said as the lights dimmed.

A short time later, it was over. The play had been a success. Julie couldn't have been more proud if they'd been her own children and felt as though her buttons would bust when people complimented the boys on their performances. Her lack of faith shamed her when she considered she had believed they wouldn't be able to pull it off.

The beautiful story never failed to touch her, from the incredible step of faith of both Mary and Joseph in accepting God's plan for them to the humble beginnings of their Lord— the joy and celebration of the wondrous birth of a Savior sent to die for the sins of the world.

Seeing the children reenact the Christmas story gave the holiday such sweetness Julie found it difficult to restrain the tears. Joey and Mari would be so proud of their boys.

The lamb had provided them with the biggest laugh of the evening. It managed to escape Luke's hold again and the entire group of children had chased after the poor thing. Finally, Luke grabbed the animal, and when the other kids left the stage, he'd remained, holding the lamb and smiling at the crowd. Marc had come out to lead him off.

Noah invited them out for ice cream to celebrate.

"Are you sure you want to do this?" Julie asked as they picked the babies up from the nursery.

"More than you know. I often join Joe and Mari for a Sunday meal. She's always kind enough to invite this bachelor to enjoy her fine cooking."

"Within the confines of their home. We could pick up something from the grocery store."

Noah shook his head. "We have to go to the ice cream parlor. They have the best flavors."

Julie gave in. "Okay, you asked for it."

He helped secure the children in the van. Julie figured the boys must be tired when they didn't make a lot of noise during the ride. Generally, the volume deafened her. "I meant to tell you I enjoyed your sermon this morning."

"Thanks. Hearing you say that means a lot."

His comment confused her. She wasn't a sermon expert, but his words had been succinct and to the point and at times she felt as though he'd directed the message at her. Had her propensity for gift giving inspired him? "You were very convincing. I certainly can see the merit of feeling salvation is a special gift."

"I pray that anyone in church this morning who doesn't know the Lord will do the same."

"Amen," Julie agreed. She followed his directions to the ice cream shop she visited many times the past summer.

"Turn left at the next light," Noah told her.

She drove into the lot and parked near the door. "We can still buy ice cream and take it home."

"What fun is that? We need sprinkles and gummy worms and all sorts of stuff to really make it good."

Julie found his response amusing. "You're a kid at heart."

Inside the small ice cream parlor, they ordered bowls of vanilla ice cream and allowed each boy to choose his own toppings. Julie opted for a dish of plain vanilla with the intention of sharing with the twins.

They held hands while Noah blessed the food. The older boys sat inside the booth, with her and Noah on the ends. The twins sat between them in high chairs. She spooned ice cream into Naomi's mouth, and when John reached for the spoon, Noah fed him ice cream. He passed napkins to the boys and the analogy Joey had once made of a family as a team came to mind. Noah had certainly been a team player during her stay.

"I'm looking forward to taking you to the cantata next Friday night."

She hesitated and Naomi grabbed the spoon, dumping the ice cream onto her shirt. Julie concentrated on wiping the child's clothing.

"You will go, won't you?" Noah asked somewhat doubtfully.

"I'm not comfortable leaving the kids," Julie told him as she fed Naomi more ice cream. "Can't we take them along?"

Noah had mentioned the idea while they were keeping the twins occupied in the fellowship hall the day before. She hadn't committed because she didn't feel right about leaving the responsibility of five children to someone else.

"The idea is to give you time away from them," Noah argued. "I doubt you'd enjoy the program if they were claiming your attention."

"I don't know. Joey said Mari wanted family to care for the kids."

"And you have. I'm sure they expected that I'd invite you out on a date at least one night while you're here."

"Maggie did say she'd babysit, but I don't want her to miss the cantata."

"She's seen it," Noah offered as he fed John a spoonful of ice cream. The toddler promptly put his hand in his mouth then rubbed ice cream on his head. "This is an encore performance. Everyone else saw the program when they did it Sunday before last," he explained as he dabbed John's hair with his napkin.

"I'll see what I can do," Julie said. "Now that I'm no longer following Mari's instructions for the holidays, I have to do my own planning."

The boys talked about the lamb as they finished their

sundaes. Noah took them to the bathroom to wash their hands while Julie picked up the trash. Noah carried John and held the door while the boys filed out, followed by Julie and Naomi. She hit the button to unlock the van doors. Noah slid the door back and the boys climbed in.

Once they were all buckled in and on the way home, Julie said, "I wanted to ask about the Good Shepherd window fund. What is that?"

"Joe wants to replace that large window behind the pulpit with a stained glass window depicting the Good Shepherd and His flock. The membership has dedicated about half the money."

"Could I offer the rest in Joey's honor?"

Noah hesitated. "I'm not sure how he'd feel about that. The intent is that the window be dedicated to the Lord."

His attitude bothered Julie. Every time she brought up the subject of donations to the church, Noah discouraged her. "And how would me giving the other half of the funds affect that? You make it sound as though I'm offering tainted money. I earn every dime I spend."

"That's not what I meant. Joe's goal is to beautify God's house. From what Joe told me, the congregation jumped on board with the idea from day one. He gave me the impression they want to provide the funding."

"It's a donation, Noah. Not a demand for a plaque bearing Joey's name."

"I'll ask and get back to you. How's that?"

"Obviously it's the way it's going to be. I just wanted to donate to my big brother's church. Why does everything have to be such a big deal?"

"I haven't developed Joe's savvy when it comes to church politics, but I don't want him dealing with problems we've caused when he gets home."

It wasn't the first time she'd heard that phrase. She had a good idea why Noah had said it at least a half dozen times.

"Joey asked you to keep me under control, didn't he?"

His guilty expression told her she'd been right on target.

"I'm trying to be the voice of reason."

"I'm perfectly capable of making decisions without the guidance of you two guys." She didn't say another word as she pulled into the turn lane and waited for the light.

"Julie, please. Don't get upset over this," Noah pleaded. "Joe asked me to help out."

"I wanna go home, Auntie Hulie."

They both glanced back at Luke.

"So do I." And she didn't mean Joey's home. She couldn't wait until her brother came home. She'd tell him exactly what she thought of his attempt to control her just before she got on her plane. Julie pulled into the church parking lot and stopped by Noah's vehicle. She left the van idling as she waited for him to get out.

"I'll help you get the kids inside," he offered.

"No thanks. I've got it under control."

"Julie?"

"Good night, Noah," she repeated, not bothering to disguise the coldness of her tone.

"I love you, Julie."

"You'll have to pardon me if I have my doubts."

He sighed and got out. She drove over to the parsonage and parked. When she opened the side door the boys spilled out and headed for the house. Julie took the twins into her arms and glanced at the open door. She'd get it later.

She heard it shut as she unlocked the front door and glanced back to find Noah standing there. Turning her back on him, she went inside and locked up behind them, turning off the porch light.

After the kids were in bed, Julie lay down for a few minutes. She couldn't rest for thinking about what had happened with Noah tonight. How could she love someone who didn't accept her as an adult capable of making her own decisions?

She wasn't looking for a replacement for her parents or her brother.

Her eyes drifted closed.

How did a cricket get into the bedroom? Julie wondered when she woke to the maddening chirp. It took a couple of minutes for her sleep-boggled mind to recognize the ring of the phone. She grabbed it up, her voice coming out as if she'd swallowed a frog.

"Hi, Jules."

"Joey, do you know what time it is?"

"Need to set your clock?" he teased.

"No, but you could set yours," she said, reaching to turn on the lamp. "You're lucky you didn't wake the kids."

"I know it's early but we're leaving for our bus tour and Mari wanted to check in before we left. How was the play?"

"They did fine."

"Can't wait to hear all about it." Before she could say more, Joey spoke to someone in the background. "We're loading up. Mari says hello and to kiss the kids."

"Joey, we've got a problem," Julie began. The static crackle of the connection cut in before she could finish.

"Can't hear you, Jules. Gotta run. Love you."

"Love you, too," she whispered to the irritating buzz of the dial tone. She flipped the lamp off and lay back against the pillows with a sigh. She'd tried to tell him about the list. Maybe she could the next time he called. That is, if there was a next time before they arrived home.

nine

Monday morning dawned chilly and wet. After breakfast, her first action of the day was to discipline Luke for flushing the list and Naomi's shoe. After much consideration, she'd decided the only way to make him understand would be to take something he cared about a great deal from him. She opted for his favorite truck.

Luke cried and pleaded but Julie placed the truck behind locked closet doors.

Later, she made sure all the kids were dressed and prepared to load them into the van. She had to buy stamps and get the remainder of her cards in the mail. She'd already left them far too long. At this rate, some of them wouldn't arrive until after New Year's Day.

The phone rang just as she was struggling to get Naomi into her sneakers. The child didn't want to wear them and kept curling her toes. Julie scooped her up and carried her into the kitchen to answer the phone.

"Hi, Julie. You have a minute?"

Surely he didn't want to discuss last night's argument. "More like ten seconds. What's up?"

"Computer problems."

She was no stranger to Cornerstone's antiquated equipment. She'd been telling Joey for months that it needed to be replaced. "What's it doing now?"

"Jean downloaded information from the Internet for one of the members and weird stuff's happening."

"Sounds like she downloaded a bug. Have her run the antivirus program to check."

"What does it look like?"

Julie sighed. Unbelievable. With all the bad stuff out there, antivirus programs and firewalls were necessities. "I'll come over."

Julie helped the children with their coats and grabbed an umbrella for the walk over to the church. One thing for certain, Joey couldn't complain about a work commute. In the office, she instructed the kids to wait in the visitor chairs while she checked out the computer. As she suspected, there was no antivirus program.

"The good news is once this is repaired, we can use the backup to restore everything." At Jean's crestfallen look, Julie asked, "You backed up the files, right?"

"Not lately. Pastor Dennis will be upset. He told me to but I forgot."

Julie felt sorry for the woman. "We'll get it running again."

"Shouldn't we take it to the shop?" Jean asked.

Julie glanced at Noah. Obviously, the church secretary didn't know Pastor Dennis's sister worked with computers.

"No need. Julie's a certified expert, Jean. Do you have the time?" Noah asked. "With the kids and all, I mean."

"Bring it to the house later. I'll check it out after they go to bed. You'll need to pick up an antivirus program." She named the one she preferred.

"Thanks, Julie, you're a lifesaver," Noah told her. "I owe you one."

"Get my tables and chairs for Christmas Day and we'll call it even."

"Already done."

"Bet you had no idea it would be a full-time job when Joey asked you to help me out, did you?" Julie asked, reminding him of his promise to her brother.

Noah grinned at that. "I'm enjoying every minute. I keep waiting for the next shoe to drop."

"You mean flush," she countered at his pun. "We're on our way to the post office. You need anything mailed?" Noah and

Jean shook their heads. "My friends will receive their cards after Christmas, but the PB and J smears will be a dead giveaway that getting them out hasn't been my top priority."

Julie felt her heart lift with Noah's laughter. She wanted to be angry with him. She really did, but she knew he'd agreed to Joey's request out of loyalty to her brother.

Noah removed his jacket from the coatrack. "I'll run to the office supply store and pick up that program. Then I can bring the computer over when you get home."

"Want to ride with us?" she invited. No sense in taking two cars when she was going to be in the vicinity anyway.

"Sure," he agreed. "Hold down the fort, Jean. God's army is marching forward to attack the church's computer virus."

"Find the last backup you did," Julie instructed before they headed out the door. "At least we can get that much restored."

They left the forlorn secretary in search of the programs Julie would need to get the computer operational. Even then, there was no guarantee the computer would work as it should. They really needed new equipment.

The rain had stopped and the boys raced ahead of them at their usual speed while Julie and Noah followed at a more leisurely pace with the twins. "Joey called early this morning."

"Was he able to help with the list?" Noah asked as he waited for her to unlock the van.

"He woke me up. I never got the chance to tell him. By the time I got around to the problem, the connection broke up and they were loading the bus for their tour."

"So what do you do now?"

"Follow the advice of a wise friend."

"Oh?" Noah said, raising his brow in question. "Which advice was that?"

Julie punched his arm. "This friend suggested I pray about the situation, which I did, and I feel the prayer has been answered."

She secured Naomi in her car seat then repeated the task

with John. She warned the children to keep their hands inside as she closed the door.

Noah reached to open the driver's door. "How did you reach that conclusion?"

"If I'd told them, they would worry. This way I worry enough for all of us and they continue to enjoy their vacation. Now I can do things my way and say the list went down the pipes. I can't feel bad about not doing as good a job as Mari if I don't know what's on that list."

Noah considered her words. "So you've adopted Luke's 'out of sight, out of mind' logic?"

"Don't tell him," Julie whispered, "but Luke did me a favor."

"You never needed the list, Julie. You've done a good job."

In that moment, she understood the importance of positive reinforcement from someone who cared. His arm rested on her shoulder, the earnestness of his expression pushing her to tears. Julie turned into his arms, her warm hug saying the words she couldn't.

The spontaneous hug surprised them both. She stepped back, laughing nervously. "I'm sorry. Being around the kids has me hyper."

"It's okay," Noah said, taking her hand in his. "A hug is one of the best experiences in the world."

"I know. The kids lavish them on me so freely that sometimes I feel overwhelmed by love."

Their gazes met and held for several seconds. The bond strengthened as Noah smiled and said, "Feel free to share the overflow anytime."

Julie climbed into the driver's seat and turned the key. She looked over her shoulder and started to back out of the driveway.

Noah pointed to the man standing at the front door. "Were you expecting someone?"

"Everyone stay put," Julie instructed. Out of habit, she shut off the engine and palmed the keys. "I'll be right back."

She ran across the yard and up onto the porch. "Hello. Can I help you?"

The way the stranger stood at an angle, shielding something from view, made Julie nervous. She felt silly when he tipped his hat in a gesture of politeness.

"I brought your cat. I know I'm early but we're going out of town so it's now or never."

Julie gasped. He'd brought the children's Christmas gift a week early. How was she supposed to keep a kitten secret for that long?

"I took care of his shots and all."

Julie glanced up when Noah opened the door. She waved him back. "Okay, Mr. . . ?" For the life of her, she couldn't remember the man's name.

"Jones. Henry Jones. Sorry, ma'am, I delivered the others today. He's the last of the litter. Might be someone would take him off your hands."

Julie quickly took the kitten into her hands, enjoying the soft, furry feel of him. "Oh, we want him!" she exclaimed. "He's a surprise for the kids for Christmas. I need somewhere to keep him until then."

"Just put him in an empty room. He takes to the litter box really well."

An impossibility in this house, Julie thought. Oh well, she had no other choice. "Thanks for bringing him by, Mr. Jones. I'm sure the children will love him."

"Merry Christmas, Miss Dennis."

Julie unlocked the door and ran upstairs to Joe and Mari's bedroom. She pulled an old towel from the linen closet and placed it on the bathroom floor. She'd shut the kitten up in there and would take care of everything else later.

When the doorbell rang again, she secured the bathroom door and hurried downstairs to find Mr. Jones at the door holding a cardboard box. "Here's the rest of the stuff you'll need right away."

Thankfully, he'd anticipated the need for a litter box. There was also a bag of litter and a scoop. He'd also included some cat toys and a bag of food. It occurred to Julie that she'd just given herself another living thing to look after.

"Thanks again, Mr. Jones."

She hurried back upstairs and set up the items, closing the bathroom door behind her.

After locking up the house, Julie realized the rain had started up again. And of course her umbrella was in the van. She ran across the yard and climbed inside, swiping the rain out of her eyes.

"What did he want?" Noah asked curiously.

Julie buckled her seat belt and said, "Tell you later. Too many ears."

૨ৱ

Noah sat with the kids in the van while she ran her errand at the post office. At the office supply store, Julie snagged a sales assistant and outlined what she wanted. She could probably get it cheaper but there was no time. Within minutes, she'd laid down plastic for three computers, software, and the necessary essentials. She even bought a phone with an answering machine and extra handsets that plugged into electrical outlets for Joey's house. No more running for the phone.

She got in the van, drove to package pickup, and jumped out to run around and open the back doors. She told the boys to move up a seat and folded down the backseat so they could stack the boxes.

Noah turned around to see what was happening. "What did you do, Julie?"

She answered him once she was behind the steering wheel again. "I took care of the problem."

"That's more than an antivirus program."

She flashed him a bright smile. "Isn't it wonderful? God provided two new computers for the church."

"God or you?"

"God used me. I've been telling Joey for months that the computer needed replacing. I got him a laptop so he can work from home when he needs to. And if the congregation doesn't want the donation, Joey can take both computers home with him. I don't think that will be the case. Once I get the old computer running again, we can set it up in your office." She flashed him a playful grimace. "I did buy you some additional memory and a couple of extra surprises." Julie turned up the heater to ward off the wet chill in the air. "Will we get snow?"

"Probably not," Noah said. "It might be interesting to see if it did snow. Jean tells me the city literally shuts down. Schools, businesses, even government offices close. She said they had a major snowfall on Christmas several years ago."

"I guess they're not prepared."

"Not much use for snowplows on the coast."

She glanced in the rearview mirror at the boys. "Matt, Marc, do you remember snow?"

They had been toddlers when they lived in Colorado. Both boys shook their heads. "Your dad used to take you guys and your mom on a sled and go down the hills really fast. Sometimes he'd crash and dump you all out. You always begged to do it again."

"Want snow," Luke announced.

"Maybe we'll have snow when your parents bring you to Denver to visit. We had so much fun making snowmen and snow angels. We even had snowball fights. I'm a good shot—always hit your dad right in the chest with those big wet snowballs."

The kids giggled and Julie told Noah about watching a program where the man turned his lawn into a Winter Wonderland. Maybe she'd call around and see if anyone had the equipment. That would certainly be a surprise.

Soon they were home. The older kids went into the living room, while Julie and Noah carried the sleeping babies up to their cribs.

"What did the man want?" he asked as he laid John down.

"The kitten I bought the kids for Christmas arrived early. Mr. Jones is going out of town."

"You bought them a pet without getting their parents' permission?" Noah demanded.

Shocked by his bluntness, Julie said, "Joey sort of gave me blanket permission."

"You said expensive gifts. I'm sure he never considered you'd bring a pet into the family."

"Why not? Pets are good for kids."

Noah shook his head in disbelief. "Do you want me to take it to my apartment until Christmas Eve?"

"It's a him," Julie said, settling Naomi in the crib and removing her shoes. The baby flexed her toes and Julie smiled at the gesture. She felt the same way about shoes. "No. Thanks, though. I hid him in Joey and Mari's bathroom. Hopefully I can keep him there until Christmas morning."

"I wonder how a cat will fit in with Matt's hamster and that aquarium in the living room. I wouldn't even think about pets if I had five children."

Had she made a mistake? Maybe she should have asked first.

Noah covered John with a blanket. "Animals do help develop the kids' sense of responsibility. Matt loves that hamster. And they love to watch the fish eat."

"True," Julie said. "I have to keep the food hidden or they'll feed them until they pop. Luke's a bit heavy-handed when it comes to sprinkling the fish food."

"You don't allow him to shake it out of the container, do you?"

Julie found his question confusing. *How else did you feed fish?*

"Mari puts a pinch of food in his hand and holds him up so he can scatter it over the water."

"I suppose I should visit Joey and Mari more often."

"Good idea. I'd better run. Should I still bring the computer over later? Jean's right about that backup. Joe's not going to be happy. He worked hard to convince the congregation that a computer would save time for everyone. I think they agreed because he told them his sister would give free advice. I hope Jean hasn't lost the church tithe records. Or the budget stuff."

"It won't happen again," Julie promised. "This one has an automatic system backup. All she has to do is stick in a CD and it does the work."

"Are you going to stick around and teach us how to use it?"

"I'll make sure Jean understands before I leave."

"Thanks, Julie," he said, kissing her cheek before he darted down the stairs.

&

True to his word, Noah showed up that evening around bath time. Luke seemed determined to take a bath with some special toy, and Julie left him searching with orders to stay out of the tub while she went downstairs to let Noah in.

One minute she was closing the door and the next, a flash of yellow tabby shot past her. Julie groaned. Luke must have gone into his parents' bathroom. "Catch him!" she shrieked.

The child bounded down the stairs. "What that, Auntie Hulie?"

"Nothing," she said, hoping he would give up and go back to search for his bath toy.

No such luck. The child ran around the room, looking behind and under chairs in search of the scrambling ball of fur. "Me find!"

Julie looked to Noah for help.

The kitten chose that moment to make his escape. Luke followed. The animal ran up the Christmas tree and she dashed after them, pushing Luke out of the way when the large tree toppled forward. The lights flickered and went out, ornaments smashing as they fell onto the floor.

"Julie?" Noah yelled, deep concern filling his voice.

Noah grabbed the kitten, handing it to Luke as he extricated Julie from underneath the tree. After she stood and he could see she was okay, Noah removed a cartoon ornament from her hair and started to laugh.

"Ho, ho, ho, Merry Christmas," she murmured sarcastically.

"I wish I had a video of that. You should have seen the look on your face when that tree fell. It was easily worth a small fortune."

"Matt, Marc, come see!" Luke bellowed at the top of his lungs as he hugged the quivering animal tightly.

Julie rescued the kitten, stroking him gently. He buried his claws into her arm when the boys bounded into the room. She'd probably have to pay for therapy. "Do they have pet psychologists?"

Noah started to laugh again.

"We got kitty!" Luke announced.

They converged around her to pet the animal while Noah attempted to set the tree back up. "I'll get something to wipe up the water," he said, disappearing into the kitchen to find a mop and bucket.

"Here, Matt, hold him gently while I help Noah clean up this mess. Don't go near the tree," she warned at the sight of their bare feet. She found a broom and dustpan and swept up the broken ornaments while Noah mopped up water.

"I take it you never secured it to the wall?"

"I'm going to see if Joey has any wire in the garage right now. Serves me right for procrastinating."

Noah started to laugh. "Julie, I'm sorry," he murmured, his mirth increasing until he bent over double. "It's so funny. That cat shot out from nowhere and ran up the tree. Luke was running around looking for him and next thing I knew you were stretched out under that monstrous tree while that stupid Santa sang in the background."

The hilarity of the situation caught up with her and Julie joined in. Luke came over and wrapped his arms about her legs, gazing up at her with innocent eyes. "Lukie, you're going to kill me before this vacation is over," she said, setting Noah off in fresh laughter.

ten

Want to go shopping tonight, Julie Joy?" Noah asked when he called about four thirty Tuesday afternoon.

He'd stuck around the previous evening to help get the kids and kitten settled in and attempted to put the tree back together while she worked on restoring the computer.

"How's it going?" he'd asked after connecting the tree to the stairs with the nylon fishing line they'd found in Joe's tackle box. He hadn't wanted to cut up his buddy's spool of line, but Julie had insisted.

"Joey won't need it again until next summer," she'd argued. "He can buy more."

After he'd finished with the tree, he pulled out a chair and sat down at the table.

"I can't believe Jean downloads anything without virus protection. She's lucky she didn't lose everything."

"She had no idea what could happen," Noah had defended. "Don't forget we don't have your computer expertise."

When it came to her work, Julie could handle everything—far different from the kids. While computers responded to her labors, the children resisted her efforts to fit them into little categories.

Luke's act of rebellion had pretty much taken care of her list-following tendencies. She would have to play this week by ear. Noah could hardly wait to see what happened.

She hit a few more buttons and smiled her satisfaction. "One hundred percent virus free. Jean will need to recreate the last three months of tithe records, though. The accounting records seem to be all there."

"That's a relief."

He'd watched her strip open the packages she pulled from a shopping bag.

"These will help some. It won't be as fast as the new ones, but I think it'll serve your purposes. I'll work on the other two tomorrow night. I need to install the programs Jean gave me and transfer the data from this one."

And now, he'd suggested they go shopping instead. "You're joking, right?"

"No way. I have shopping to finish."

"You didn't wait to mail your gifts, did you?"

She knew him well. "No. I learned that lesson with Mom's birthday present. I mailed them the first of December. These gifts are for people here."

"Noah, I don't know. The kids—"

"Get back on the horse, Julie," he encouraged. "You can handle them. Besides, I'll be there to help."

"You promise?"

"You take Luke and the twins and I'll handle Matt and Marc."

"What if I want Matt and Marc?"

"Okay, I'll take the twins and Luke."

There was a moment of silence. "On second thought, I'd just as soon keep an eye on Luke myself."

"So you'll go?"

"Yes. But only because I have shopping to finish as well. We can go after I feed the kids."

"But I'd planned to treat everyone to dinner."

"Too late. Dinner's already on the table. We're having hot dogs and baked beans if you'd care to join us."

"You made baked beans?"

"Actually, Mrs. Allene sent over a casserole. I think she's seeing too many takeout deliveries over here."

"I'm on my way."

"I'll set a place for you."

When he knocked on the back door, Julie waved him in.

He washed up at the kitchen sink and sat in Joey's chair. She spooned a serving onto his plate and took her seat at the opposite end of the table.

After he blessed the food, Noah took a bite and said, "This is great. You're not eating the casserole?"

Julie grimaced at the suggestion. "Joey made beans a staple in our diet. I can barely tolerate them."

"You don't know what you're missing." He scooped up another big mouthful and savored them. She smiled when the boys did the same.

"Just consider it a bigger serving for you guys," she suggested.

Noah grinned. "Can't argue with that logic. Mrs. Allene's baked beans are the best I've ever eaten. They disappear so fast at the church dinners that I rarely get any."

"Does she have a secret family recipe or something?"

Noah shook his head. "I'm pretty sure it's in the church cookbook. Mari has a copy, I think. So how was your day?"

"We're falling into a routine. I get the children up, dressed, and fed. They play. I do chores and feed them lunch. They play. I do more chores. They play."

Noah laughed at her droll description. "That's quite a routine."

"I can't imagine how Mari has time for church work, friends, or anything else, for that matter. The kids take so much time."

Noah spooned more casserole onto his plate and added more to Matt's when he held his plate out. "Her friends are mothers, too. They visit while the children play. One day Mari and I were talking about getting everything done and she told me that routine doesn't have to be set in stone. She said that no matter how much she likes to keep a clean, orderly house, it's more important to spend quality time with the children. She says what goes undone today waits until tomorrow."

"But is that practical?"

"Sure it is. Think about it, Julie. If you don't do small loads of laundry today, you do larger ones tomorrow. If you don't run a partial load in the dishwasher, it's a full load tomorrow. The dust layer on the furniture is only slightly thicker."

"What about a working wife? Letting chores back up like that would make things difficult. Particularly with children."

"Froo, Auntie Hulie," Luke said, bringing his plate over to show her.

She took the plate, wiped his mouth, and excused him to wash up.

"I'd rather my wife not work while the children are small, but if she did, we'd find a way to make it work."

"I like my work. I mean. . . I want to work."

Noah found her response interesting. Did Julie see herself in his life? In the role of mother? "Then you will. It might make things more difficult but not insurmountable."

"That doesn't sound like a minister's point of view. Joey doesn't want Mari working. He feels her place is in the home."

"Don't you think they discussed it and then made the joint decision that she would stay home?" Noah asked.

"I suppose," Julie said with a shrug of her shoulder.

"They feel their lives run more smoothly because she's here taking care of their family and home."

"So you agree that's the best way?"

Her vagueness bothered him. "I didn't say that. It's a problem to overcome when it arises."

"Problem?"

"Situation," he corrected. "If you married me and we made a decision to have children, we'd come to a mutual decision on how to raise them. Who knows? Maybe I'd take a leave of absence and care for them."

"You'd do that?" Julie asked, obviously taken aback by his comment. "Even if the congregation frowned on it?"

"What kind of man would I be if I didn't put my family before the opinions of others?"

"They'd look down on me for forcing you to make that decision."

Noah fixed his gaze on her as he said, "Supporting each other in whatever we choose to do is what love is about."

"My job is probably more flexible," she said, shaking her head the moment the words left her lips. "Why are we having this conversation, anyway?"

Julie's abrupt turnabout didn't surprise Noah. He knew she was confused and he wanted to clear that confusion from her mind.

One by one, the boys finished dinner and were excused. "Wash your hands and visit the bathroom," Julie told them. "We'll be leaving soon."

Noah started gathering plates and scraping them. "Why don't you take care of the kids while I clear this up and then we'll head out?"

&

The shopping excursion went well. Julie found that trading off responsibility with Noah made everything easier. If she wanted to look at something, he kept the children together and she did the same when he shopped.

After finishing at the shopping center, they drove over to the Christian bookstore.

"I'm glad you had this idea," Julie told him as they waited for their gifts to be wrapped. "I'd all but decided to write checks and stuff them into Christmas envelopes. You really think these are okay for the Sunday school teachers?" she asked, studying the small daily devotionals they'd picked out.

"They're perfect."

After loading the kids, they piled the packages in the back.

"Anywhere else you need to go?" Noah asked.

"Home. The children are tired."

"Me, too," Noah agreed. "I only have a couple more gifts to buy. You never told me what you'd like."

"I have everything I need."

"Everything?" he repeated, his eyebrow lifting in doubt.

"I'll let you know if anything comes to mind."

"Just remember to allow others to experience the same joy of giving."

~

Life in the Dennis household settled to a dull roar over the next couple of days. On Wednesday Matt went off for a play day with his friend, and Julie left the other children in day care for a few hours. She finished her shopping in record time.

She'd had a busy week. The church computer system was operational again. From her conversations with Jean, she knew the woman had been busy trying to put everything back together. Some information had been lost, but Jean had reconstructed the tithe records from the envelopes stored in the church office. She'd mentioned retyping some of Joey's sermon notes, but Julie suggested she wait until he returned and see if she should proceed.

Jean had faithfully backed up the system every day and admitted to loving the new, faster computer. No members of the congregation appeared to mind Julie's contribution.

The kitten had settled into the household, avoiding the children whenever possible. So far, she had fished Puff out of the aquarium twice. Hoping to curb the kitten's fishing tendencies, she'd visited the pet store today to purchase a lighted cover for the huge container—but not before the two fish went missing.

The funniest thing was Puff's reaction to Matt's hamster. Secretly, Julie had dubbed the hamster Houdini. A master at escaping his cage, she had lost count of the number of times they had hunted for the hamster since she'd been at the house. Knowing the hamster was loose didn't exactly thrill her, either, but the kitten was terrified of the hamster and climbed to the highest points possible to hide.

Julie picked up kid's meals for everyone and headed for home. Merline was pulling up with Matt when she arrived. After lunch Julie decided to use Naomi and John's nap time to wrap gifts in the bedroom. She looked in on the older boys and found them playing.

The missing Christmas presents still troubled her. She felt clueless as to how to handle the situation. The temptation to pick up the phone and call Joey was strong, but the feeling he expected her to call kept Julie from dialing the emergency number. She wasn't ready to admit defeat yet. If the gifts didn't show up of their own accord, she supposed they could keep the children busy until Joey retrieved them Christmas morning. If only she'd studied Mari's list more thoroughly—but how could she have known it would disappear down the drain?

Christmas dinner plans were well under way. She'd placed orders for turkey and spiral sliced ham. She'd visited the bakery for breads and pies and met Avery Baker. As Noah suggested, he'd tried to tempt her to order cakes and when she admitted that Natalie Porter had donated two already, he'd provided a red velvet cake and fudge brownies. She'd asked about his plans for dinner and invited him to join them.

The guest list remained a puzzle. Finally, she'd asked Noah for a list of people who were alone for the holidays and invited them. So far, over half had phoned to say they'd love to come and asked what they could bring.

Julie told them to bring their specialty dish. There would be far too much food, but everyone could take plates home with them, and she felt certain there would be a few homebound church members who could benefit from a meal, as well.

She felt good about the plans. Christmas dinner would be served at four o'clock to give Joey and Mari time to spend with the kids and rest a bit before the guests arrived. After morning services, Julie planned to return home to organize things.

She placed several of the larger gifts in bags and topped them off with tissue paper. Julie liked the design on the paper she'd picked for the children. She finished the roll and tied on the ribbons before going to check on the boys. The twins were still asleep and she found Matt and Marc playing in their bedroom. There was no sign of Luke.

The older boys only shrugged when she asked where he'd

gone. Julie turned the house upside down. Her cries resounded across the backyard as she continued to search.

Noah raced across the church parking lot, pulling on his leather jacket. "What's wrong?"

"Luke," Julie said breathlessly. "I can't find him."

"When did you last see him?"

"He was playing with Puff in the bedroom about fifteen minutes ago."

"Then he hasn't gone far. What about Matt and Marc?"

"They don't know."

"Auntie Julie," Matt called from the back door. "Luke said Puff wanted to go for a walk."

Fear filled her as she looked at Noah. "Surely he didn't leave the house without permission."

Noah called the child's name again and again with no response. After another few minutes, he said, "We'd better call for help."

Julie dialed 911 and explained the situation. Within minutes, an officer arrived. He looked familiar but she couldn't place where she'd seen him before.

"Pastor," he said with a nod of his head.

"Burt," Noah greeted him, reaching out to shake his hand. "I'm glad they sent you. You know Luke and he knows you. This is Pastor Joe's sister, Julie Dennis."

As the officer asked questions, the church lot began to fill with vehicles as volunteers arrived to aid in the search.

Julie lingered by the back door. "He can't have gone far," she insisted. "It's only been minutes."

"Come sit down," Noah urged, taking her arm and guiding her to a chair.

"If he's chasing the cat, there's no telling how far he's gone," the officer said. "We'll fan out and cover the area around the house."

"I'll get my coat," Julie said.

Burt shook his head. "I need you here, Miss Dennis. In case

Luke finds his way back home on his own."

Fear planted its seed deep and wide in her mind as she considered the ramifications of not finding Luke. She hugged her arms against her body, fighting back the tears. "I managed to mess up the one thing Joey asked of me. I should have realized there's a reason they didn't have a dog or cat. If I hadn't bought that stupid kitten, Luke wouldn't be lost now."

"You can't say that for sure," Noah argued. "Luke could have disappeared for any reason. There are better ways to spend your time than blaming yourself for something you can't change."

"Like what?"

"Prayer for one thing. It can't hurt to send up a few on Luke's behalf. And the older boys need to be reassured."

She pressed her hands to her mouth. "I'm not fit to take care of children."

"Julie, stop," Noah demanded, pulling her close. "God is taking care of Luke. Don't doubt that."

Burt stepped closer and held out his hand. Julie took it and Noah's as he led them in prayer, seeking Luke's safety and Julie's comfort.

"We'll find him, Miss Dennis."

She offered Burt a weak smile. "Thanks for your help."

Time dragged by. When three o'clock passed with no sign of Luke or Puff, Julie paced the kitchen. "It will be dark soon and it's getting colder by the minute. I should be out there searching."

Her panic resulted in Noah reaching for her hand. "You should be here. When they find Luke, he's going to need your comfort. Let's pray again."

Naomi started to cry and Julie went to comfort the baby. "She's so clingy. I think she knows something's wrong."

Julie relished the comfort of the toddler's delicate frame against her body. If only she could do the same for Luke.

Tears trailed down her cheeks. "Oh, Noah, I vowed Luke wouldn't get lost again while I was in charge. How will I ever tell Joey I lost his son twice? What if something terrible happens to him?"

"Nothing's going to happen. God is in control. Why don't I go check and see how things are going?"

Julie felt so alone after he'd gone.

God, please keep Luke safe, she pleaded silently as she rocked Naomi. *He's too little to know the dangers of the world.*

Matt came to stand by the chair. "Auntie Julie, can we have some milk?"

Glad for something to occupy her, Julie took them into the kitchen and filled glasses and cups and placed cookies on a plate.

After they started to eat, she stared out the window over the sink, seeking signs of the search. There was no one in sight. Noah still hadn't returned.

When the children finished their snack, Julie sat at the table with them and doodled along the edges of the menu for Christmas Day. They all needed something to do.

She set oranges in front of Matt and Marc with a bowl of cloves. "Help Aunt Julie," she told them, demonstrating how to push the spice into the oranges for the wassail she planned to make. Maybe their efforts wouldn't be as neat and perfect as they could have been, but the activity would help them all pass the agonizing time.

When the back door opened, Julie grabbed a towel and wiped her hands, demanding anxiously, "Noah, what did you find out?"

"They brought in tracking dogs. Do you have something Luke wore recently that they can use for scent?"

She ran upstairs and used his pillowcase to retrieve the pajamas he'd left underneath his pillow that morning, hoping the scent of oranges and spices wouldn't transfer from her hands to the garments. She handed them to the dog handler outside. The man waved the clothing under the dog's nose and spoke to the animal.

"Will it work?" she asked.

"We hope so, ma'am."

When the animal began to bark and strain at the leash, Julie broke down again. Where could he be? Injured or lost in the woods behind the house? Why hadn't she checked on them sooner?

Noah squeezed her hands. "It's going to be okay."

"Are there any signs he's out there?"

"They seem to be going around in circles. Burt found some small prints he feels are Luke's."

"He doesn't know the way back."

"Believe, Julie. Believe God will bring Luke home."

She grabbed a paper towel and rubbed her eyes. "I'm trying. Did I tell you Joey asked if I'd assume guardianship if something happened to him and Mari?"

"Would you?"

"What choice would I have? There's no chance I'd allow them to be separated."

"Is that the only reason?"

"No. I'd do it because they're my family and I love them."

The clock chimed the hour.

"But when I consider what a mess I've made in less than two weeks, I don't even want to think about what I'd do to them in a lifetime."

Noah patted her shoulder. "You've been a good parent. Let's keep things normal." He joined the boys at the table and helped with the oranges.

The atmosphere in the room seemed almost depressing. All the kids were abnormally quiet. She missed Luke's chatter.

Another few minutes passed and Julie started dinner. All Luke's favorites—just in case.

There was a knock at the door and she recognized the officer from earlier. He removed his hat as he stepped inside. "Luke's been found, Miss Dennis."

"Thank You, God!" Julie shouted. "Where? Is he okay?"

"Fine. He and his kitten were fast asleep in a little valley not too far from here. Prepare yourself. He's rested and full of his adventure. Talking about how his cat escaped during their walk and he chased him."

An overwhelming distaste for the cat struck Julie. "You don't know a family who wants a kitten, do you?"

The man shook his head. "Can't say I do. Seems to me Luke deserves his pet after getting himself lost because of Puff."

His radio sounded and he responded. "They're bringing him to the house now."

"Thanks so much."

"Glad to help. The EMTs are here. They need to check Luke over just to be sure he's okay."

"Can they bring their equipment inside?"

The officer nodded and went back outside.

Julie turned into Noah's arms. "Thank God. I've never been so frightened."

"I could tell," Noah said as he curved the palms of his hands about her face and kissed her gently. "I love you, Julie Joy."

"I love you, too."

She pulled away and walked over to the storm door to wait. Her heart pounded when she saw the officer approach, holding Luke's hand. Puff hung underneath the child's arm as Luke talked excitedly. When they stepped inside, Julie dropped to her knees and hugged him close.

"Puff ran away, Auntie Hulie."

Julie hugged him tighter and cried softly.

He squirmed in her hold. "You're squishing me, Auntie Hulie."

She let go and reached for the kitten. "Give Puff to me. These gentlemen need to make sure you're okay."

Julie held the kitten against her chest and rubbed her hand over his fur as she waited for the EMTs to examine Luke. The child asked a million questions as they checked his vitals.

"He's fine, Miss Dennis. Nothing a good meal, a hot bath,

and a good night's rest won't fix."

"Hungee, Auntie Hulie."

Julie almost smiled. At least getting lost hadn't hurt his appetite. "Dinner is nearly ready. Go wash up and tell your brothers."

After the room cleared, Julie burst into tears. Her shoulders trembled as she sobbed in relief. The sobs soon turned into hiccups.

"Oh, honey, everything's okay," Noah soothed, wrapping his arm about her shoulder.

"I was so afraid they wouldn't find him."

"I know but he's home and none the worse for his adventure. That's a blessing."

Julie pulled back and wiped her cheeks, pushing the kitten at Noah. "Here. Take Puff. Put him in the cage in Mari and Joey's bathroom for now. I can't bear to look at him."

He cuddled the animal. "It's not his fault, Julie. He only did what animals do."

She didn't want to blame the kitten for Luke's disappearance. "It's my fault and I have to fix it. I should never have brought a kitten into this house." The noise of the boys whooping and hollering as they charged down the stairs reminded her she had work to do. She rubbed her eyes again. "I need to finish dinner."

"Don't make your decision out of fear. Why don't you sit and relax for a bit?"

"No," she said with a shake of her head. "I have to feed the children. Everything has to be normal."

Soon they were all gathered around the table, the scene as normal as every other night when they dined as a group. Luke went on and on about how Puff ran away until Julie felt she might scream.

"Luke, you know better than to leave the house without permission," she said finally. She could not allow him or the other boys to think this type of behavior would be accepted.

"Wif Puff, Auntie Hulie."

"Puff is not a responsible adult, Luke. You know you're not allowed to leave the house without permission," she said sternly.

Luke's expression crumpled but Julie refused to give in. Protecting him was her job and she wouldn't let this happen again. "You must understand how dangerous leaving the house alone can be. How do you think I'd feel if something happened to any of you? It would break my heart. And your mom's and dad's."

Noah attempted to intercede for the child. "I'm sure Luke is sorry he went out without permission."

"No, I don't think he understands," Julie argued with a firm shake of her head. "Luke, you will not leave the house again without an adult. Do you remember what your dad said? If you misbehave, he expects me to punish you. Do you understand?"

He sniffed and nodded his head.

"That goes for all of you. Does everyone understand what I'm telling you?" Julie's gaze shifted from child to child and she waited for their response.

They all nodded.

"And, Luke, you cannot play with Puff again until I tell you it's okay. Understood?"

The child looked as though he wanted to cry. He nodded slowly.

"Why don't you take the kids into the living room?" Noah suggested. "I'll straighten up in here and bring you a cup of cocoa."

Julie felt as if she'd drop from sheer exhaustion. The older boys played at her feet while Naomi and John toddled about the room. Luke cuddled at her side.

"You know I love you, don't you?" she asked softly.

He nodded.

"Promise you won't go outside by yourself again?"

"Torry, Auntie Hulie."

She kissed the top of his head. "Me, too, Luke." *I should have taken better care of you today.*

Noah soon joined them, handing Julie the promised cup of cocoa.

The evening hours stretched on as they watched a Christmas special on television. "Okay, guys, time for bed," Julie announced. "I have a surprise planned for tomorrow," she blurted.

Four sets of eyes focused on her.

"What are you planning, Julie?" Noah asked.

She had arranged for them to have snow the next day. After calling for information, she'd hired a company to turn the backyard into a veritable snowy playground.

Not as good as a good old-fashioned snowfall, but the kids would enjoy the experience. Granted the snow wouldn't last long as the outside temperatures warmed up, but the memories would last forever.

"Just wait and see."

"You make me afraid when you talk like that. I never know what to expect."

"Keep 'em guessing. That's my motto."

Noah lingered after the children's bedtime and Julie couldn't decide whether he was concerned that anxiety might overcome her again or hoped she might spill the beans about the surprise.

When she started nodding off on the sofa, he stood and said, "Guess I'll head for home and prepare for the big surprise."

Julie's eyes felt so heavy as she struggled to her feet. "Good idea. Get plenty of rest. You're going to need your energy."

He pulled on his jacket. "Now I'm truly nervous."

"Don't worry," Julie reassured with a mischievous smile. "I have complete faith you can handle this."

Noah kissed her cheek. "You rest, too. It's been a stressful day."

"Definitely an incident I don't care to repeat. Only two more days until Joey and Mari return. Thank the Lord."

"Thank the Lord, indeed," Noah said, clasping her hand in his. "I'm grateful He provided this time for us to be together."

"Thanks for being here for me," Julie told him. "Especially today."

"Where else would I be?"

In her mind, the span of miles between them seemed an almost insurmountable issue, but in his presence Julie experienced overwhelming love for him. How could she make this work?

She waved good-bye and locked up the house for the night. Upstairs, she checked on the kids before heading off to bed. When she opened the bathroom door, Puff meowed in objection to being locked up all evening.

Julie opened the cage and picked him up, stroking his soft fur as she walked back into the bedroom. "I'm sorry I did this to you," she whispered. His body rumbled against her. "Noah's right. It's not your fault."

When Julie put Puff on the floor, he immediately sank his claws into Mari's comforter and climbed up to curl into a ball at the foot of the bed.

She had a strong suspicion Joey was going to kill her for this one. How could a decision that had seemed so simple at the time be so wrong? When she'd seen the advertisement for kittens in the newspaper, it never occurred to her that having one would be anything more than a good experience for the children. Now she understood the burden she'd placed on her family and had no idea how to change the situation.

eleven

The following morning, Noah zipped his leather jacket closed and blew on his hands as he waited on the steps of the Dennis home. "Cold out here," Noah exclaimed when Julie opened the door.

"Oh, come on, Noah. Spring in Denver is colder than this."

"What's that noise?"

"Come see," Julie invited.

Noah followed her to the kitchen and glanced out the window. He could hardly believe his eyes. "Snow?"

"Surprise!" she said, laughing at his confused expression. "There's more than one snowball out there with your name on it. I'm so happy the temperature dropped last night. The snow will last longer."

A good night's rest had obviously helped. Noah shook his head and said, "There's no end to what money can buy."

Julie punched his shoulder. "Even I know better than that. And you know as well as I do that this manmade stuff is nothing compared to the real thing. Money has its limitations.

"Everything is in God's hands. Money can't buy health or happiness. When the doctors diagnosed Mari, I'd have given every dime I had to keep her healthy for the sake of Joey and her children. I knew that would be God's choice. And I'm so thankful everything turned out for the best. When I got the news, I had this overwhelming feeling that if God needed to take anyone, it should be me. Mari had so many more reasons to live. So many people who needed her."

"Thank God it wasn't you," Noah said, the impact of her words making him ache.

"I've never been as relieved as when the doctors gave Mari

the all-clear. I love her so much," Julie admitted.

Noah wrapped his arms about Julie and hugged her fiercely. "And I love you."

About ten thirty, the children were playing in the living room when one of the men she'd hired knocked on the back door and said, "We're ready when you are, Miss Dennis."

"Thanks." She walked into the living room. "Let's get your coats, hats, and gloves. We're going outside to play."

"Don't want to," Luke told her as he continued to roll a tiny car around the rug.

"Come on, Luke," Julie pleaded. She wasn't in the mood for his rebellion today. "You'll like this surprise."

"Wanna pway car."

"Fine," she snapped. "You can nap on your bed while everyone plays in the snow."

"Snow." He jumped up and grabbed the coat Julie held. After two failed attempts to pull it on, she held it for him to slide his arms in and then turned him around to zip the coat closed.

"My do," Luke objected, pushing her hands away.

While she admired his attempts at self-sufficiency, Julie longed for the days when baby Luke had allowed her to do things for him. She handed him his hat. "Put this on. I'm going to get John and Naomi. Don't leave the house," she warned.

When she released them into the enclosed backyard a few minutes later, the boys went wild with excitement. They were everywhere, kicking through the snow the men had mounded here and there. Matt, Marc, and Luke laughed uproariously when Julie nailed Noah with a snowball right away. When he came after her, she started to run and slipped. Noah rubbed a handful of snow in her face.

Julie accepted his hand and stood. She brushed her clothes off and when he walked away, she quickly formed a snowball. "Noah!" she called.

He looked up and the snowball splattered against his chest. He grabbed two handfuls of snow and squeezed them into a weapon of his own. As he approached, Julie pulled Matt in front of her as a shield. "You wouldn't hit an innocent child with that, would you?"

"Spoilsport."

He handed the snowball to Matt, who immediately turned and tossed it at Julie.

She grabbed a handful of snow and reached for the child. "Joseph Matthew Dennis, you're going to be sorry!"

Over in the churchyard, the kids had stopped playing and congregated at the fence to watch. "Let them come play," Julie told Noah.

He hesitated for a few moments before he pulled a cell phone from his pocket. Julie waited expectantly as he spoke to the center director. "Okay, thanks, Mrs. Hill. I'll let Miss Dennis know."

"Are they coming?"

"She says most of the kids aren't dressed warmly enough to play in snow. She's afraid they'll get sick if they get their clothes wet. Plus they only have a few more minutes of recess."

Julie felt saddened by his news, but realistically she knew the center director was right.

The machine continued to turn water into snow while the boys pushed a large snowball around the house, stopping at the gate to the fence. While Noah finished the huge snowman, Julie went inside for a colorful scarf and a carrot for his nose.

"You think the congregation will say something about us placing this snowman near the church?"

"I doubt he'll last long enough for them to complain."

About fifteen minutes later, Luke came over and wrapped his arms about her legs. "Cold, Auntie Hulie."

She gathered the shivering child into her arms and squeezed him. "Time to take this party inside before everyone gets sick," she called to Noah.

"I have to get back to work, too. Thanks for the memories, Julie Joy," he added. "Only you would have thought of making your own snow day."

"I enjoyed myself."

"What time should I pick you up tonight? The cantata starts at seven. I thought we might go out to dinner before. What about five?"

"I'll check with Maggie and see when she's available."

"Call me."

After the children had warmed up, Julie sat on the sofa with them all around her. "Did you enjoy the snow?"

"I remember snow at our old house." Matt jumped from the couch and ran across to tug a photo album off the bookcase shelf. He thumbed through the pages. "See?"

Julie studied the photo of Joey, Mari, Julie, Matt, and Marc hugged up to a gigantic snowman. "I'd forgotten that. You guys were so little."

"Where me, Aunt Hulie?"

"You weren't born yet, Luke."

"What borned?"

Oh no, she thought. She didn't plan to touch that one.

"You weren't there," Matt told him.

Out of the mouths of babes. Why hadn't she thought of that? She turned the pages, enjoying the journey into the past.

"Daddy likes this picture," Matt volunteered, flipping the page open to a photo of Julie and Joey with their parents. "He says that's Grandpa and Grandma Dennis."

The picture, which had been taken the last winter before their parents' deaths, brought tears to Julie's eyes. Joey had been home for Christmas when that huge snowfall had come. "Mom liked to make figures out of the snow. Our snow couple had children and a dog. Mom wanted to build them a house but Daddy said she'd used up all the snow."

The boys giggled and Julie regretted that they'd missed the opportunity to know their father's parents. They were such loving and giving people. They would have loved Joey's children so much. At least they'd had a close relationship with Mari's mother. She wondered if they missed their grandmother Edy as much as their mother did.

"Well, guys, I have to get busy. Lots of work to do before Sunday. I need you to entertain yourselves for a while."

Luke raced for the stairs.

"Where are you going?"

"Find Puff."

Dread shot through Julie. "Have you forgotten what I told you about Puff, Luke?"

He came over and leaned against her leg. "No forget." She ran her fingers through his hair. "Pway with twuck, Auntie Hulie?"

That seemed a good alternative to playing with the kitten. She opened the closet and took down his favorite. At least it wouldn't entice him out of the house. "We'll work on your gifts for your parents after I finish in the kitchen."

Julie had visited the craft store to pick out items for the boys to make stepping-stones for their parents. She'd gotten Joe and Mari a mosaic bench for the backyard and figured they'd enjoy the stones while they sat and watched the children play. Later, she'd prepare the concrete and put it in the pans so they could decorate them with the various stones they'd chosen.

In the kitchen, she dialed Maggie's number and waited for the ring. Noah had overcome Julie's objection to leaving the children by having Maggie insist on babysitting. "Hi, it's Julie. Are we still on for tonight?"

"I'm looking forward to it. What time?"

"Noah wants to go to dinner around five. Is that too early?"

"Not at all!" Maggie exclaimed. "I love spending as much time as possible with the children."

Julie kept busy all afternoon, not giving herself time to think about spending the evening with Noah. She hesitated to call it a date. It had been months since they'd shared anything more than a phone call. She felt comfortable with him after having spent so many hours of the past two weeks in his company, but she knew Noah wanted to know where they were going as a couple and she didn't have a clue.

twelve

Julie slipped her diamond stud earrings on before she ran downstairs to open the door to Maggie Gregory.

"You look nice."

She looked down at the sparkly red Christmas sweater she'd paired with a black skirt and boots. When she'd packed for the trip, she'd almost left it behind but had second thoughts. It was too pretty not to wear. "Too bright for church?"

"Not at all. The color is perfect for Christmas."

"Thanks for doing this for me. Who's keeping the nursery tonight?"

"Whoever's next in rotation. We take turns so no one gets burned out. If you don't mind, I like to take the children over to visit Mrs. Allene. She hasn't been feeling well but she wants to give them their gifts."

Julie felt bad that she hadn't checked on the elderly neighbor. The woman had been so kind to Julie during her stay.

They walked into the living room to find toys spread everywhere.

"You guys know the rules," Julie said. "Put everything away but one toy. Now please."

The boys picked them up, dumping them into the baskets where Mari stored them. Julie admired the way her sister-in-law had trained the boys to pick up after themselves. They even tried to make their beds and put their dirty clothes in the hamper.

"Is it okay to take them over to Mrs. Allene's?" Maggie asked again.

"Of course. I should have checked on Mrs. Allene. Let me get her gift from us."

Julie had wrapped the gift just yesterday and knew exactly where she'd placed it underneath the tree.

"She knows you're busy with the children."

"Are you sure she's up to the commotion? And be sure to keep an eye on Luke," she warned.

Maggie patted Julie's arm. "Don't worry."

She tried not to but it was difficult. The woman was probably far better equipped to care for them, but they were Julie's responsibility. "My cell number is on the pad by the phone. It's long distance but call if you need me." She dropped into the armchair. "I'm so used to taking care of them, I'll probably try to spoon-feed Noah."

They both burst into laughter. The doorbell rang and Julie chuckled again when she let Noah in.

"What's so funny?"

"Nothing," she told him, winking at Maggie as they stepped into the living room. "Where are we eating?"

Julie wasn't familiar with the restaurant Noah named.

"Try their salmon. It's fantastic," Maggie suggested. "I'm not expecting you back until late. Have fun."

"Not too late," Julie told her. "There's a lot to be done tomorrow."

"Just concentrate on having fun tonight, Julie," Noah told her. "You can worry about the rest tomorrow."

Noah helped Julie with her coat and took her arm as they walked out to his car. He opened the door and the small interior seemed cramped after traveling in the van. "I'm glad you agreed to come tonight."

"I'm looking forward to the cantata." Julie found herself enjoying the outside decorations as they drove through the neighborhood. She really should take the children sightseeing. "I love Christmas. Everything is so sparkly and beautiful."

"Like you. You look great, Julie. But then you always look beautiful to me."

Warmth flooded her face. Noah had always been generous

with his flattery. She knew she wasn't anything special, but it was nice to hear someone liked her appearance.

"I can't tell you how happy I am that we have this time alone."

The dashboard lights provided Julie with enough glow to study Noah's profile. "We've had time together."

"The kids were always just a short distance away. Your mind was on them more than on us."

"I can't help that," she defended.

Noah glanced at her. "I'm not criticizing you, Julie. I only ask that you forget about them for a few hours and just let it be us together."

Us. Was she prepared for "us" time? Over the past few days, her anger toward Noah had slowly evaporated, leaving behind the realization that nothing had changed. When she left South Carolina in a few days, she'd leave a major part of her heart behind.

Her love for Noah and her family would make going back to Denver even more difficult, but she'd deal with it again, alone, just as she'd done before. Well, not exactly alone. She would stand firm in her intention to return to church and give God a portion of her time. Tonight, she'd give Noah her undivided attention.

"I wish I could have taken you to see the Christmas entertainment available in the various theaters," Noah said as he helped her from the car.

"This is fine. I'm looking forward to the cantata."

The restaurant he'd chosen was cozy and romantic. A white cloth draped their table. Candles provided the subdued lighting. The waiter handed them their menus and after learning they weren't interested in wine, asked what they'd care to drink. Noah surprised Julie by requesting iced sweet tea.

"It's the beverage of choice at the church," he said at her questioning glance. "I've grown to love the stuff since I moved here."

Mari must give it to the kids, too. She'd wondered about that when she asked Matt if he wanted juice or milk and he'd said tea. Julie hadn't developed a taste for the beverage and opted for water with lemon at most meals. She had stuck with juice and water for the children, as well. *No kids allowed*, she chastised silently. "Tell me what's good."

Noah pointed out the items he'd enjoyed on previous visits. "Let's order different entrées and share."

She nodded agreement. They'd done that often when dining out.

"Do you still go to our restaurant?" Noah asked.

Julie shook her head. She didn't go anyplace that reminded her of them.

"I always loved their spaghetti. No one can make it like Jose."

Julie laughed with him. It never failed to amuse them that their favorite Italian restaurant had a chef named Jose. She recalled the time Noah had asked to meet him. It turned out Jose was the son of an Italian mother and Spanish father and had learned to cook the foods of two cultures.

"Did you repaint the condo yet?"

Julie had threatened to repaint the place about a thousand times since she'd met him, but she'd never gotten beyond paint charts. "I'll probably hire someone to do it soon."

"I can't believe you're still living with that mauve paint in the living room. You hated it."

She despised the color. It went okay with her white furniture, but she preferred more earthy tones. "It defeats the purpose if I paint it before I get new carpet."

"I thought you were going to redo the hardwood floors?"

"When I have time."

"It does have a way of getting away from us, doesn't it? I can hardly believe I've already been here six months."

Julie didn't have any problem believing it. That's exactly how long she'd put her life on hold. She hadn't redone the condo simply because there was no one around to appreciate it but her, and she spent so much time at work that she'd convinced herself it would be a waste of time. She hadn't worked nearly as many hours when her family and Noah were around.

"Ready to order?" their waiter inquired after placing their drinks and a basket of bread on the table.

Julie glanced at Noah and back at the menu. "I'll have the Cajun grilled salmon," she said.

"Sounds good. I'll get a seafood combo. That way you can sample the variety they have here on the coast."

Noah passed her the basket after the waiter left to place their order. "Try these."

She eyed the strange-looking bread doubtfully.

"They're called hush puppies. It's fried corn bread. Try one."

She found it tasty.

The moonlight glimmered off the ocean just outside the restaurant. Even in the darkness, the vast amount of water on the horizon fascinated Julie. "Looks different at night. I've had a hard time adapting to the humidity here."

"Be glad you're visiting in winter. The summer heat leaves me breathless at times. I miss the mountains."

Julie nodded. Making comparisons between the two states was something she found herself doing often. The South Carolina sky seemed so much paler than the sapphire blue of the Colorado skies. Here, flat land stretched out as far as the eye could see. In Denver the mountain ranges were always in the western horizon. She looked forward to going home. "My vacation has gone so quickly. I can't believe tomorrow is Christmas Eve. The New Year will be here before we know it."

"Plan to make any resolutions?"

Julie sipped her water and set the glass back on the table. "To get to church more often. Maybe this will be the year to redecorate the condo."

"Or sell it and move here."

His comment surprised Julie. "I'm sure Joey doesn't want his pesky baby sister around interfering with his life. Having me miles away is probably the best thing that's ever happened to him."

"Why would you think that?" Noah asked, his intensity startling her.

Julie fiddled with her silverware. "He gave up too much for me already. I wouldn't dream of intruding on his family."

The waiter set their salads on the table. Julie placed her napkin in her lap and poured the honey mustard dressing over the greens.

"You're Joe's family, too, Julie. He'd never resent you."

"I'm his sister, Noah. That's not the same as a wife and children. He has plenty going on in his life without having me underfoot. Joey did his time. He deserves a break."

"You know it's not like that," he objected. "Even when you live in the same community, you don't see each other that often. You have your work and different friends and a place of your own to keep you occupied."

"I already have that in Denver," she pointed out.

Her response clearly exasperated Noah. "And I'm trying to say I want you in my life. You've already said you don't do long distance. So where does that leave us?"

"In different places."

"Why are you so closed-minded about this?" Noah demanded.

Julie laid her fork on the salad plate. "I'm being realistic. Your life isn't your own. You belong to God. What happens when you get a church of your own? Do you expect me to pull up roots and follow you to another new area? Be separated from Joey and Mari and the kids again?"

"I would if you were my wife. I love you, Julie."

"You loved me so much you walked away from us, Noah. Pardon me if I'm not able to trust that it wouldn't happen again if God called you. You're anticipating a future that can take you anywhere. I didn't ask you to change your life on a whim. Don't ask that of me, either."

"I want to share that future with you. Home is not the building, Julie. It's the place where you're happiest with the people you love. We could be happy if you'd just open your mind to sharing your life with me regardless of where we are. I realize I made a big mistake when I didn't discuss my intentions with you before I left. I didn't do it to put you out of my life. I did it so I'd have a future to offer you."

The waiter arrived with their entrées and the conversation paused as they sampled their foods.

"Try this," Noah offered, spearing a shrimp with his fork and holding it out to her.

"That's good," she agreed. "Want to try my salmon?"

They sampled each other's food until they were full. When the waiter asked if they cared for dessert, both quickly refused. "I'll have to remember that seafood sampler next time I come here."

"So you're planning on there being a next time?"

When Noah tried to pick up where they'd left off, Julie glanced at her watch and said, "You'd better finish your coffee. It's already after six and we need to get to the church a few minutes early to get good seats."

&

"What's the answer, Lord?" Noah asked later that night as he rested in his recliner searching his Bible for answers.

He believed he'd stated his intentions fairly clearly to Julie. He wanted to marry her. How would they ever progress if she wasn't willing to even consider the possibilities?

After dinner they'd driven to Cornerstone and found seats. He'd enjoyed hearing the cantata again. Noah felt confident Julie had enjoyed herself, as well. He'd seen tears in her eyes during the more moving songs, and she'd commented on how good the program had been several times when he'd walked her home.

Then when they'd arrived at her front door, she'd thanked him for a wonderful evening and said good night. He'd intended to plead his cause further. Maybe even give her the ring that burned a hole in his pocket.

Noah wished Joe were here now. He could use his friend's counsel. Joe understood Julie. Perhaps he could tell him how to reach her.

"I don't want to let her go again, Lord," he spoke aloud. "I believe You have guided her back into my life for this purpose, and I'm ready to accept the role of husband and provider. How do I make her understand?"

Wait.

"How long?" Noah asked.

His gaze dropped to the Bible. Isaiah 42:16 leapt off the page at him: "I will lead the blind by ways they have not known, along unfamiliar paths I will guide them; I will turn the darkness into light before them and make the rough places smooth. These are the things I will do; I will not forsake them."

"Thank You, Lord," he whispered. God knew the answer. Noah only had to wait on His timing.

❧

When Noah had asked if he could come in, Julie knew he wanted to continue their discussion. She'd explained that it was late and she had lots to do the next day. Her entrance set off the singing Santa. "That thing is getting on my nerves," she grumbled as she stopped to hang her coat and bag on the rack.

"I cut him off until after the kids went to bed," Maggie admitted. "They kept setting him off."

"I'll be happy to leave him here with Joey and Mari. Don't be surprised when he shows up in a yard sale."

"Did you enjoy yourself?" Maggie asked.

"I did," she agreed with a broad smile and a nod. "The cantata was wonderful. Thanks for making it possible. How were the kids?"

"Pretty good. I took them to see Mrs. Allene. She gave them gifts and fed them ice cream and cookies."

Julie winced. She didn't envy Maggie five kids on a sugar

high. "I'm sure they enjoyed themselves."

"Mrs. Allene did, too. She loves those children."

From what Mari had told her, their neighbor had been widowed several years earlier. "What about her family? Doesn't she have children? Grandchildren?"

"A son. Dillon. He's an engineer somewhere overseas."

"He doesn't visit her?"

"Not often," Maggie said, shaking her head in dismay. "It's sad. I don't think he even realizes his mother won't be around forever. Her health has declined so much this past year, but I know she hasn't told him."

Julie curled up in the armchair and pulled a chenille afghan over her legs. "Why don't you call him?"

"It's not my place. I love Mrs. Allene like my own mother. I'd never do anything to upset her."

She felt confused. Their parents had never minded telling Joey when he was overdue for a visit. "Why would suggesting her son visit upset her?"

"She says he's busy. She puts his needs before her own."

Julie remembered that much about her parents. No matter what she and Joey did, they had stood by them. Joey had stood by her as well. "Maybe Joey could give him a call. Sometimes men understand each other better."

"I'll see how things go. If she doesn't get better soon, I'll make the call myself. I couldn't bear it if she left this world without seeing him again."

"You're close to her, aren't you?"

"When I bought my house, Mrs. Allene came over and welcomed me to the neighborhood. She invited me to visit Cornerstone. Thanks to her, I found my church home. She's been a true friend and I love her dearly. Now tell me about your date."

"It was nice."

"That's such a mundane word for a beautiful couple. Noah obviously cares a great deal for you."

"He says he loves me."

"You don't believe him?"

Julie fingered the fringe on the afghan. "He loves God more."

"As he should. Putting God first in your life is first priority."

Julie felt overwhelming selfishness as she tried to make Maggie understand. "But he walked away from us."

"Did he ask you to come with him?"

"Noah never committed to anything. After he left and I realized how much I loved him, I considered following him here."

"Why didn't you?"

"Joey said Noah was popular with the ladies at Cornerstone."

"We all like him, but I wouldn't say he's pursued anyone romantically," Maggie offered.

"I know that now, but I took Joey's statement to mean Noah had moved on with his life."

"Why would Pastor Joe make such a statement?"

"I intend to ask him when he gets home. But there's more to the story than that. When Noah received the job offer, he made his decision without even asking my opinion. If he truly loved me, he would have cared what I thought. I believe he feels I'm too young. But I'm old enough to know my own mind. I stopped being a child the day my parents were killed."

"So you want to marry Noah?"

Julie blew out a stream of air and dragged her hand through her hair. "I love him but I don't know that I can give up everything that's important to me to follow him as he serves the Lord."

"You can if God asks it of you." That wasn't the advice Julie wanted to hear. "Loving someone makes you want the best for them. And when you love them enough, there's nothing they can ask of you that you'd refuse. Your brother and Noah have a very important calling. They need women they can depend on to support them in an arduous task."

"Joey certainly has that in Mari. I could never be half the woman she is."

"God doesn't want you to be like Mari, Julie. He made you unique."

"That He did," Julie agreed. "I'm a one-of-a-kind, break-the-mold and throw-it-away sort of woman."

Maggie laughed. "I'd say you need to search deep within yourself and determine how much you care for Noah. If you love him as much as I think you do, you'll figure out a way to put God first in your life and in your relationship. Otherwise, you're destined to live an empty life. Believe me, I know how that can be. Careers and friends don't replace the need to have a special person in your life."

"You never married?"

Maggie shook her head. "I kept telling myself 'one day,' but life got away from me. I'm fifty years old."

"That's not too old," Julie protested.

"I'm pretty set in my ways. I doubt I'd ever find anyone who'd have me at this point in my life."

"I don't believe that for a minute. You're a wonderful person, Maggie Gregory, and any man would be blessed to have you for his wife."

The woman's cheeks colored. "Thanks, Julie. I'd better be getting home. I have a twelve-hour shift at the hospital tomorrow."

"On Christmas Eve?"

"Sickness never takes a day off. I work tomorrow and I'm off until the following Wednesday."

"Will you join us for dinner on Christmas Day?"

"I plan to come over for a while. I thought I might take a plate over to Mrs. Allene and stay with her for a bit."

"We can get a wheelchair and bring her over for dinner if she's up to it," Julie suggested.

"We'll see," Maggie said as she prepared to leave. "Pray about you and Noah. God will lead you if you let Him."

She scrambled to her feet and followed Maggie to the front door. The Santa started singing and she quickly turned him off before he woke the kids. Maggie laughed at her quick reaction.

"Thanks for tonight, Maggie—and for the advice. I promise to pray about my situation if you'll do the same. I think God has a Mr. Right out there for you, too."

"We'll see. Thanks again for letting me spend time with the kids tonight."

"Joey and Mari are blessed with their family," Julie agreed, feeling melancholy as she considered not seeing the children again for months. "I'm going to miss them so much."

"Then perhaps you should consider making some life changes to accommodate all the people you love so much."

Perhaps I should, Julie agreed as she locked up for the night and headed upstairs.

thirteen

Julie set the alarm clock with intentions of rising early and getting a few chores out of the way before the children woke, but when it went off, she slapped the snooze button and closed her eyes again. After three times, she rolled out of bed and headed for the shower.

Tilting her head back beneath the spray, Julie rinsed the shampoo from her hair and considered the restless night she'd spent. Thoughts of her date with Noah and then Maggie's words had made sleep impossible. Would she really have an empty life if she opted not to change? Surely not.

Last night hadn't been the night to lose sleep. She had far too much to finish today. Christmas Eve. Julie could hardly believe the end was in sight. Tonight she had planned a party to commemorate Jesus' birthday. At first, she'd invited Noah and Matt's friend, Jeremy, but the list had grown steadily into a good-sized party.

Between tonight's party and Christmas dinner, Julie accepted it would be a hectic day. After getting the children dressed and fed, Julie loaded them into the van and started picking up the things she'd ordered. *Too bad the day care is closed on Saturdays,* she thought after the third stop.

The boys squabbled in the back until her head throbbed in earnest. Matt seemed determined to make Luke cry. "Leave him alone, Matt."

"He's touching me, Auntie Julie."

"Don't touch him, Luke."

"My twuck, Auntie Hulie."

"Give him his truck."

She swung the van into a parking lot and got out to separate

142

Matt and Luke. "You know better, Joseph Matthew," she said sternly.

"He wouldn't share."

"You should have brought your own toy."

She checked her list and started the van, driving to the store where she'd ordered the turkey and hams. Thankfully, that was her last stop.

Back at the house, she fed the children lunch. "I need to get organized for the party tonight," she said in her no-nonsense tone. "If you can't play together, you'll have to take a nap. I don't have time to referee."

Once she started cleaning the house, the children seemed determined to test her. The twins woke after a short nap, whiny and demanding her attention. The older boys fought until she put them all in a time-out. The only way she'd get anything accomplished would be to hire a babysitter. Julie grabbed the phone and dialed Noah's number. "Do you have Robin's number?"

"Good afternoon to you, too."

"I'm sorry. I have tons to get done and the children refuse to behave."

"Want me to come over?"

Julie didn't hesitate to agree. Her load was too heavy to shoulder alone. "Yes, please. I need two interruption-free hours to finish."

"I have a couple of things to pick up and then I'll be over."

"Could you pick up some cranberries? The grocery store was out and I wanted to make a cranberry salad for tomorrow. The boys were fighting and I completely forgot about them."

"No problem. See you soon."

Julie couldn't believe the children's behavioral turnaround once Noah made his appearance. He took them out to play while she worked inside. She lingered at the window, watching him laugh as the children raced around him.

Destined to live an empty life. Maggie's words struck home.

Julie considered the fear of loss she'd dealt with when her family and then Noah had moved away. Could she deal with that emotion each time Noah's job required them to move on?

She saw Luke battling the blow-up figurine. Julie took a step toward the door and stopped when she saw Noah lead the child away. She returned to washing the vegetables.

Empty life. Her life these past two weeks had been full. Did she want to go back to a life devoid of family? Noah's declaration of intent certainly offered promise for their future.

Just as My Son's birth offered hope for a dying world.

One tiny baby boy, born to die for a world of sinners He loved, had made such a difference. The thought made her concerns seem petty and shallow.

What was she really afraid of? Noah loved her. She loved him. Perhaps her inadequacies in terms of being a good minister's wife? Noah deserved someone like Mari. Someone who could help him carry through on his promises to God. Not a stubborn, opinionated woman subject to assumption and anger.

Julie arranged the veggies on the tray and covered them with plastic wrap. She was placing them in the fridge when the doorbell rang. She hurried to answer.

Natalie stood there holding a large cake box. "Hi," she said, pushing it into Julie's hands. She laughed at the Santa's movements as he sang. "Be right back." She ran back to her car and returned with a second box and a basket. "Merry Christmas. I brought you some of my specialty candies for the party. And some cookies for the children. Where are they?" she asked, glancing around the room.

"Noah has them outside. They were driving me crazy."

"Nice guy," Natalie said as she carried the treats into the kitchen for Julie.

"He is," Julie agreed. "Would you care for coffee or some eggnog?"

"I have to run. I need to finish my deliveries and get to the airport. My friends are flying in tonight."

They placed the items on the kitchen table and Julie walked back through the living room with her. "Come by later if you get a chance."

"We'll try."

"Thanks for everything, Natalie."

"You're welcome. It's been great having you here, Julie. I hope to see more of you in the future."

They hugged and Natalie hooted when the Santa started singing again. "That thing is a riot. Merry Christmas."

Julie repeated the greeting and closed the door. She took her coat and hat off the coatrack and headed outside. Noah had the twins in their swings and alternated pushing them. He smiled when she stepped up alongside and began to push John's swing.

"Finished?"

"Finally. Looks like they've run off some of their excess energy."

"Would you like to go out for an early dinner?"

"Where did you have in mind?"

He named a chain restaurant Julie enjoyed. She released John's seat belt and removed him from the swing. "Sounds good. Come on, guys. Let's get ready for dinner."

&

They arrived to find the restaurant filled with holiday revelers. Tables filled with family and friends visiting and exchanging gifts.

"Thanks again for your help," Julie told Noah once they were all seated. "I was close to the end of my rope."

"You were frazzled," Noah agreed. "Too much planning stressed you out."

"Probably. I shouldn't have done the party tonight. Tomorrow will be hectic enough."

"At least the party won't last long. After everyone leaves, you can put the kids to bed and put your feet up."

"Don't tease me," Julie joked. "I haven't relaxed in two weeks.

No reason to think I'd start tonight. Now tomorrow night is a different story."

That night as the house filled to capacity, Julie found herself enjoying this group of strangers. The guests devoured eggnog, cocoa, sodas, cookies, birthday cake, and assorted snacks. Then they gathered around the piano to sing carols.

When Noah suggested they take their show on the road, her guests bundled up and walked over to the church. They stood out front, caroling and passing out candy canes to the sightseers who drove by to view the nativity. A few parked and joined in the festivities.

Robin had offered to stay at the house with the twins, and Julie took the older boys with her. They'd raced around with their friends and after half an hour, complained about the cold. She finally called good night to Noah and the others.

After she'd closed the door behind Robin, Julie breathed a sigh of relief. Soon the kids would be in bed and tomorrow she'd be free.

When the phone rang around eight thirty, Julie decided one of the guests had forgotten something.

"Miss Dennis, this is Geneva Simpson. I called to ask when you'll be picking up the children's gifts. Mari has them stored in my attic."

Julie almost whooped with joy. "Oh, thank you, Mrs. Simpson!" She explained the catastrophe with the list, adding, "I had no idea where to look."

The woman laughed. "That Luke is a character."

"What time do you go to bed?" Julie asked. "I need to get someone to stay with the kids while I run out to your place."

"I can have my husband bring their things over after the children are in bed," Mrs. Simpson volunteered.

"I'd be eternally grateful."

"We're glad to help."

Julie felt overjoyed. "What are you doing for dinner tomorrow?"

"Chester and I will eat at home."

"Come eat with us. We're celebrating Jesus' birthday in fellowship. Several church members have agreed to come."

"We got your invitation but we didn't want to be a burden."

If she only knew what a blessing she's just become, Julie thought. "I can't tell you the weight you've lifted from my shoulders. Please say you'll come."

The woman agreed and promised to have her husband bring the gifts after nine thirty. Julie's heart and steps lightened as she ran upstairs to settle the boys in bed. They were restless, anticipating the morning, and it took longer than usual for them to fall asleep.

After reading them the Christmas story, Julie turned off the lights and sat with them in the glow of the night-light. After much tossing and turning, Matt and Marc gave in to their exhaustion and drifted off. She sat on the edge of Luke's bed. "Want me to lie down with you for a while?"

He bounced on the bed making room for her, and Julie cuddled him beside her. "Are you excited about Mommy and Daddy coming home tomorrow?" she whispered. His head bobbed up and down as she fingered his soft hair. "I know they'll be happy to see you, too. Will you miss Aunt Julie?" Luke nodded again and a knot formed in her throat. "I'm going to miss you guys so much when I go home."

"Why you go, Auntie Hulie?"

She wanted to cry. "Because my home is there."

"You stay with me."

"And where would I sleep?" she asked.

"Sweep with me."

Julie smiled at his generosity though she couldn't imagine the two of them in the twin bed. "I love you, Luke."

Amazingly enough, all five of the children had fallen asleep by the time the headlights indicating the arrival of their personal Santa flashed on the house.

Julie ran downstairs to help Mr. Simpson. "You truly are

Santa," she exclaimed as they piled boxes about the room.

"The missus and I added a few things," he said. "We never had any little ones of our own. We love these children so much."

"They are a lovable bunch," Julie agreed. "I know Joey and Mari appreciate your help. Providing for five children can't be easy."

Her gift to the family had been a computer and several programs intended to help the children's educational potential. She'd even added high-speed Internet access for the year. If they decided to homeschool Matt, the computer would prove helpful. Besides, they could e-mail her to save on telephone calls.

Still, her expensive gift wasn't comparable to those of this one couple who had probably used a bit of their pension income to provide for her brother's children.

"I'm glad you and your wife are joining us tomorrow."

"Geneva said we'd be coming. Can I help you with anything else?" he asked as he rolled a third bicycle into the room.

"You've helped more than you realize," Julie said, smiling brightly as she thanked him again. She wished him a good night and closed the door. Her spirits sank a bit as she approached the gift piles. Why hadn't she checked before Mr. Simpson left? Without hesitation, she went to the phone. "Noah, help."

"Julie, what's wrong? The kids?"

"They're fine. We got a blessing of sorts. Mr. Simpson just delivered their gifts, but nothing's assembled."

"Think Mari covered that on her list?"

"Probably. What am I going to do? I can build a computer from the ground up, but even with a complete set of instructions, I know nothing about toy assembly."

"I'm on my way. Maybe you should put on a pot of coffee."

"Thanks, Noah."

❧

Noah arrived a few minutes later and Julie led the way to the unassembled red wagon that lay on the living room floor.

Julie plopped down on the floor and tried to fit two pieces together, groaning when they fell apart. "Why didn't Joey take care of this before he left? He promised Mari would handle everything."

"How do you know they didn't?" Noah challenged. "Maybe part of the plan was to ask someone to put this stuff together before tonight."

Julie passed the wagon instructions to him. He checked off the various parts to make sure they had everything they needed. "Where's the tool box?"

"I'll get it," she offered, jumping up off the floor.

"You can run but you can't hide," Noah teased at her eagerness. "Don't forget the coffee."

Julie grumbled a lot to begin with, but as things began to fall into place, she felt a great sense of accomplishment. Her role in the children's Christmas had expanded beyond her gift-buying tendencies.

"Tap that spot gently, Julie," Noah requested as he held the handle in place.

"Like this?" she asked, blinking away tears when she managed to pound her finger. Noah howled with laughter.

Holding her throbbing finger protectively, Julie shushed him and said, "It's not funny."

"I'm sorry. Give it to me."

She held out her hand.

"The hammer, Julie," he suggested, his grin still in place when he took a moment to kiss her battered finger.

One tap and the piece slid into place. "There, that's finished," he said, using the handle to push the wagon away. "What's next?"

"At least the bikes are assembled."

"I don't recall Joe mentioning bikes for the boys," Noah commented.

"You don't think the Simpsons bought them, do you?"

Noah shrugged. "Probably. Matt and Marc often sit with them during services."

"But it's too much."

"God rewards the faithful," he told her. "I don't know how the kids can sleep. I always remember being too excited. Every year, I kept trying to peek to see if Santa had come. What about you? I bet you were worse than me."

Julie nodded. "I put out cookies and milk and begged to sleep on the sofa. Then I fell asleep before Santa arrived and woke up in my bed. I always believed he carried me upstairs before he left."

"I'm going to miss you," he began.

"Me, too," Julie said as she unpacked a box containing a small racetrack. "Even though I'm home, I suffer homesickness until work overwhelms me and I don't have time to miss everyone."

"Stay."

Her head jerked up. "I have my job. My condo."

"Sell the condo. Find a job here. You did a great job with the office computer. I'm sure you could find work."

The possibility of freelancing had occurred to her more than once.

"Once Joey and Mari come home, there's no reason for me to stay. They have each other and the children. They don't need me getting in the way."

"I need you." Noah dropped down on one knee before her. "I've prayed about us for a long time. And I'm confident God has shown me you're the one."

"I'm not," she objected, pulling back from him. "I'm too opinionated to be a pastor's wife. You'd never get a church with my big mouth getting you into trouble."

Noah laughed. "Maybe in time we'll both learn to temper our tongues and seek God's guidance before we speak. That doesn't mean I want to wait to make you my wife. I'm ready to settle down. To be blessed with a wife and children."

"I wouldn't want more than a couple of children," Julie objected.

"And maybe God will see fit to give you that exact number. He knows the plans He has for you. But if He gives you a dozen, you could handle them, Julie Joy. Children are a gift."

"I need time, Noah. I can't make this decision right now. It would be more emotional than logical."

He took her hands in his, his loving gaze meeting hers. "Love is an emotional attachment, Julie. It's having your heart, mind, and soul agree that you can't live happily without the person you love. Take all the time you need. I'll wait for your answer because I love you."

"When Joey said you were popular with the ladies, I thought. . . Well, I believed he meant romantically. I was heartbroken that you could forget me so easily when I loved you so much."

"Why didn't you ask? I never had eyes for anyone but you, Julie Joy. I never issued or accepted a dinner invitation or did anything to lead any one of them to believe I was interested.

"You think I walked away and didn't look back? It felt like I drove the entire way to South Carolina looking over my shoulder. But I had the hope that one day we would live happily ever after. To tell the truth, I don't know that I could have left you if it hadn't been for being close to Joe and Mari and hearing how you were doing."

"I didn't date either, Noah. I wrapped myself in my work to the point that I ate, slept, and breathed computers. I didn't want to go anywhere or do anything that reminded me of you."

He stopped working on the track. "That's why you stopped going to church?"

Julie picked up the cardboard pieces that dotted the floor. "It wasn't fun anymore. Sure I knew people, but everyone I'd connected with had left the church."

"God didn't."

"I know that now. If I'd trusted Him, I'd have gotten my

answer sooner. Now I'm praying and seeking His guidance for my life. There's something I need to share with you."

Fear crossed Noah's expression.

"The real reason I'm hesitant to say yes is because I'm afraid I can't handle the pain."

"What pain?"

"The desertion, Noah. Having Joey and his family move away tore a chunk of my heart out. And when you followed, I felt devastated. And when I think about how our life together would force me to accept constant separation from the people I love. . . Well, I'm not sure I could handle that."

"I can't promise you won't ever leave people you love behind, Julie. But I can promise no one will ever love you more than I do. I've grown from our separation, too." Noah laid down the parts and concentrated on making her understand. "When Joey first suggested I cover for him, I thought here's my opportunity to prove myself invaluable to Cornerstone. Instead, I haven't done anything I wouldn't have done if he'd been here. Well, one thing," Noah corrected. "I got to spend more time with his beautiful sister."

Julie felt her skin warm. "Thank you. I guess you spent so much time shadowing me and making sure I didn't cause trouble that you didn't have time to make your mark."

"I trusted you to do right, Julie. I never doubted you. All I did was voice my concern and you cared enough to protect me as well as Joe."

"That's my problem. I don't know how to handle this life. I can't imagine being closely examined by a congregation."

"I can," Noah said softly. "Look at what you've done. I've seen nothing but your willingness to share with others."

"Oh, that's nothing," Julie said.

"It is something," Noah objected. "You took time off to care for the kids. You invited people to share Christmas dinner. You encouraged others to use their God-given talents. Those are all things a pastor's wife would do. You're a fine Christian woman, Julie Joy Dennis."

"I've had good role models. Attending church has helped me realize what I've been missing. I'm moving God to the top of my priority list."

He held out his arms and they hugged. "I can't tell you how thankful I am to hear that, but I hope you'll consider changing your place of residence."

Julie wanted to say yes—to make a new life with him. But could she be the woman he needed her to be? "I love you, Noah."

"Enough to marry me?"

"Oh, look at the time!" Julie cried when the clock chimed the hour. "You're a lifesaver, Noah, but you're going to be exhausted tomorrow. I mean today," she said upon seeing the hands had crept past three. "Merry Christmas."

"I'll be okay. It's not the first all-nighter I've pulled. You didn't answer my question, Julie."

"I don't have an answer."

"I told you I'd wait and I will, but remember families are their own circle of love. Friends complement that circle but it starts with the family. You and I would be the start of that family, and wherever we are, we'd always have each other to depend on. You've been on my heart and mind every day we've been apart. We'd better get this job completed before the kids come downstairs."

They finished assembling the small race car track, and Noah spent several minutes watching the cars whiz around it.

Around four, Julie heard Naomi's cries on the baby monitor she'd purchased. She suggested Noah take a break and went to care for the baby. She returned to the living room to find him fast asleep in the recliner.

"Bless his heart," she whispered to Naomi. After the baby fell asleep, Julie laid her on the sofa and returned to the assembly.

"Why didn't you wake me?" Noah asked when he woke about an hour later.

"You needed to rest. You have to preach this morning. I'm nearly done here."

He allowed his gaze to drift about the room. "So this is what Christmas Eve is like for a parent. Spending the wee hours making sure everything is taken care of."

Julie tucked Naomi's baby doll into the toddler-sized stroller. "Joey worked his way through college doing assembly work. Called himself Mr. Fix-It."

"I didn't know that."

"Stick with me, Noah. I can tell you all sorts of stuff about Pastor Joey."

"I'm not going anywhere," Noah said pointedly. The clock chimed six. "Speaking of Pastor Joey, I'd better head for the airport."

"Are you sure you're okay to drive?"

"I can get through the day on that nap."

She walked him to the door. "You were right," Julie admitted. "The list didn't matter. Everything turned out fine."

"We can do all things through God who strengthens us."

"You sound like a pastor," Julie teased.

"Good," he said with a satisfied smile. He cupped her face and kissed her gently.

"Noah," she called as he started out the door, "thanks for everything. Be careful."

After he left, Julie took Naomi upstairs. She came back down to add her gifts to the rest and finished organizing the room. The nativity scene sat on top of the console television, and Julie smiled as she thought of the kids' reactions to her attempt to put baby Jesus in the arrangement when they had placed it there almost two weeks ago.

"Not before Christmas," Matt had insisted until she put the figurine back in the box and stored it away.

Julie left the tree lights burning and lay down on the sofa. What an experience it had been. She would miss the kids but most of all she would miss Noah. What a friend he'd been in her hours of need. Despite his own full schedule, he'd never refused her assistance.

Noah had proposed. Excitement filled her at the possibility of becoming his wife. Her hopes plummeted just as quickly. Marrying Noah would bring so many changes to her life.

I'll miss everyone so much. Julie felt weepy at the thought of leaving everyone she loved behind.

"Father God," she prayed. "Thank You for my family. Please return Joey and Mari safely to their children. Help me strive to be a better witness for You. The gift You gave the world over two thousand years ago is truly the most wonderful gift of all.

"And, God, give me the right answer to Noah's proposal. I accept that with Your help I can be the right wife for him, but the human side of me argues the point. Give me a clear answer as to what You would have me do.

"And as always, thank You for loving and caring for me as only a loving father can. Amen."

fourteen

Wake up, Jules. Santa's brought what you wanted most for Christmas."

She stretched and offered up a sleepy smile. "And what might that be?"

Joey extended his arms and grinned. "Your beloved brother and sister-in-law, of course."

So much for her plans to be dressed and have a breakfast feast prepared. She snuggled against the sofa pillow and murmured, "Good, now you can worry about those little menaces you left with me."

"Were they that bad?" Mari asked, appearing concerned.

Julie tilted her head toward Joey. "They're his kids. What do you think?"

"I told Joey it was too much to ask of you."

Julie captured Mari's hand. "I had the time of my life. Did you enjoy your trip?"

"Oh yes. We have so much to tell you," Mari added, looking more animated that she had in some time. She glanced at the Christmas tree and back at Julie. "It's huge."

Julie pushed her feet to the floor and sat up. "There's a story behind that."

"And that lump of ice near the fence?" Joey asked.

"There's a story. . ." Julie and Noah said together, breaking into laughter.

"In fact, Julie could write a storybook," Noah said.

"I assume we still have five kids?" Joey teased.

No thanks to Luke's efforts to lose himself, Julie thought. But that was another story. "Five kids, two less fish, one hamster, and a kitten. Puff ate the fish, by the way. He's upstairs with the boys now. I meant for him to be a surprise but Luke let the cat out of the bag."

"Bathroom," Noah corrected.

Julie bared her teeth at him. "Mr. Jones went out of town and brought the kitten by early. I hid him in your bathroom but Luke wanted his bath toys and let him out."

"Then Puff, as he's now known, ran up the Christmas tree and toppled it on Julie," Noah added.

"Oh!" Mari cried, touching her hand to her chest. "Were you hurt?"

Julie tapped Noah's arm and whispered sternly, "You weren't supposed to tell that part." She looked at Mari and said, "Nothing but my pride. The tree's tied to the stairs so no one else will get attacked by that giant."

Joey laughed loudly and Mari shushed him.

"And whose bright idea was it to get a cat?" Joey inquired.

"You did give me carte blanche."

Her brother's incredulous look was a clear indicator of his thoughts on the matter. "So you got a cat?"

"Admittedly, not the smartest decision I ever made. I'm willing to do whatever it takes to rectify the situation. I can try to find him a new home before I leave. And if that doesn't work, I'll take him back to Denver with me."

"The children would be devastated if you took Puff away now," Mari said. "Besides, I've always wanted a kitty."

"He's a handful," Julie warned. "I didn't tell the boys he ate their fish."

"I suppose it's a trade-off of sorts. One new cat, two less fish," Joey said with a shrug. "So what's the story on the tree?"

Julie eyed the monster in the corner with more than a little disdain. "Matt picked it out. He insisted his mom would let him have this tree. You should have seen Mr. Simpson's face when they loaded it on the van."

"I wish we had a picture," Joey said.

Mari looked puzzled. "Matt knows I never let them choose the tree."

"They've taken me on a wild ride with all the things they claimed you'd allow."

"What about the list? I thought I'd covered everything."

Julie glanced at Noah and then back at her family members. "Luke flushed the list Saturday night. He threw Naomi's shoe in on Sunday morning to hold it down."

"He did *what*?" Joey demanded.

"He had his reasons," Julie defended. After all, he was only three. What did he know about adult fears? "We survived and that's all that matters."

Mari appeared near tears. "I missed my babies so much. I need to see them."

Joey watched his wife race up the stairs before turning back to Julie. "She got so homesick I thought we were going to have to turn around and come back. Then after a few days with no calls, she started to enjoy herself."

"There were a couple of times I thought I'd have to call."

Noah squeezed Julie's hand. "She did a great job, Joe."

"I don't doubt it for a minute." He looked around the room. "Jules, I'm seeing all sorts of new contraptions about my house."

"Remember your promise. There's not one thing here that doesn't benefit the entire family. Noah did his best to keep me under control."

Joey glanced at his friend. "She guessed?"

Noah nodded. "About the tenth time I said I didn't want you coming back to problems we'd caused. Just accept the gifts in the spirit they were intended, Joe," Noah advised. "Julie's made the best of a challenging situation."

Noah's comment captured her brother's attention. His gaze fixed on her. "Not too bad, I hope?"

"Let's just say you're indebted to Noah for life," Julie warned.

"What about you?" Noah asked with a loving smile. "Don't you owe me, too?"

Julie pointed at her brother. "You did the favor for him." Then she grinned. "Actually, I couldn't have survived this without you."

"We make a good team."

Julie nodded agreement, forgetting about Joey as she and Noah shared the moment. "The best. You're going to be an excellent father one day."

"You'll make an excellent mom."

"I hate to interrupt this mutual admiration society meeting, and I can't really say what kind of parents you two will be until after I check with my kids, but Mari and I are obliged to you both. We needed the vacation."

"And now I need one," Julie said, bursting into laughter when she glanced at Noah. "Maybe I'll stick around for another week so you can wait on me hand and foot."

"Yeah, right," Joey said. "Stick around and I'll take Mari on another vacation."

"No way, brother dear. You've had your time. We'd better sort these presents before the children come downstairs."

Julie explained how the gifts had only been located late last night. "If anything's missing, we'll have to handle it later."

They had just finished when Matt appeared at the top of the stairs holding Luke's hand. The sound of lively little boys racing down the stairs echoed throughout the house.

"Marc, Santa came!" Matt bellowed as they burst into the room.

The room became a hub of activity as the boys scouted out the gifts.

"Boys, calm down," Mari instructed when Marc brushed past her on the stairs. She carried the twins. "Daddy has to read the Christmas story first."

"Wait," Julie ordered. "I want to get this on video."

She picked up the camera from the end table. The scene before her stole Julie's breath away as she looked at the image on the small screen. Just like when they were children and their parents carried out their traditions on Christmas morning, her brother's family now did the same.

Joey sat on the sofa with Mari at his side, Naomi in her lap, and John squeezed between them. The older boys sat on the floor at his feet. He held the Dennis family Bible open to the story of Jesus' birth. Tears filled her eyes.

Noah came to sit on the chair arm next to her. "Go ahead," she directed after adjusting the camera to record this Christmas morning.

The beauty of the story filled their hearts as Joey read of that wondrous birth so long ago.

"Luke, it's your year to put the baby Jesus in the manger," Mari said.

No one seemed the least bit concerned that he was going to handle the tiny porcelain nativity piece.

"Where is Jesus, Auntie Hulie?" Luke asked.

Julie passed the camera to Noah and went to rummage in the closet where she'd stored the box. She handed it to Luke and once she saw his cautious handling of the figurine, she understood. Carefully, he made his way to the arrangement and laid baby Jesus into place.

"Let's pray," Joey said as he stood. "Heavenly Father, we come to You on this blessed Christmas morn to say thank You. Thank You for giving us Your Son, our precious Lord Jesus. Thank You for the love that surrounds us."

Julie glanced at Noah when he took her hand. She smiled softly and bowed her head again.

"Thank You for each and every member of my family and for our dear friend, Noah. Thank You for the bounty of gifts. We know that no earthly gift can ever match the wonder of what You've done for us. Please help us to be worthy of Your gift. Mari and I thank You for each of our precious children and for Your daily watch over them. As parents, we fully understand the sacrifice You made for us by allowing Your Son to die on the cross for our sins. And thank You for being here for Julie in her time of need—for giving her the strength to carry on in a momentous task. In Jesus' name, we pray. Amen."

A chorus of amens filled the room. The adults smiled when Luke jumped up and shouted, "T'ank You, God." The child turned to hug his father, and Joey swung him up into his arms. "So, how did Auntie Julie do as a mommy?" he asked.

"Auntie Hulie bestest Christmas mommy ever," Luke announced.

Her brother's love reached across the room to engulf Julie. "I knew she would be."

"You might change your mind when you know the entire story," she offered dubiously. Joey and Mari would probably never ask her to babysit again once they heard what had happened to Luke.

"They're safe and happy, Julie. That's all that matters. Hey, guys, let's see what you got for Christmas."

The children dashed for the tree. Joey and Mari joined them, making certain each child had a package to open.

Teary-eyed, Julie glanced at Noah.

"He's right, you know," Noah agreed. "No matter what happened, you kept going. You never gave up."

"At times, I wanted to," Julie admitted softly. "That's when I called on God and He sent you over to help out."

Noah kissed her hand. "I couldn't stay away." He took a tiny gift-wrapped box from his pocket. "You never did say what you wanted for Christmas."

She stripped away the paper and snapped the box open.

The lights of the tree twinkled in the lovely solitaire diamond. Julie gasped and placed one hand over her mouth.

"I want you to understand the depth of my commitment. I want to marry you, Julie Joy Dennis. I want you with me wherever we are. I want a family with you. I need you to stand by me in the pulpit as I minister to my flock."

"Oh, Noah, that's the part that scares me most. A minister's wife needs to have a calling as well. What if I let you down?"

"Are you a Christian, Julie?"

"You know I am."

"Then you have a calling. You're a disciple for our Lord Jesus Christ. You already give everything within you to those you love and I love you just like that. I called my mom this morning and asked her to pray that you would accept. Please say yes."

"Are you sure? Do you realize what you're taking on?"

Noah's smile broadened as he nodded slowly.

"Yes then, Noah. I don't ever want to leave you again."

He hugged her tightly and removed the ring from the box then slid it onto her finger.

"Hey, you guys forgot the most important piece of decoration," Joey called, smiling as he held mistletoe over Mari's head and kissed her soundly.

Noah held out his hand. "May we borrow that, Joe?"

Julie leaned toward Noah and their lips met in the sweetest kiss they'd ever shared.

"Merry Christmas, Christmas mommy," Noah whispered.

fifteen

New Year's Eve

As the music segued into the bridal march, Noah's gaze fixed expectantly on the sanctuary door and he tugged at his suddenly too-tight collar. Julie stood there in her mother's gown, looking even more beautiful, if that were possible. In a few minutes, she would become his wife. Noah could hardly believe the progression of events that had taken place since she'd accepted his ring.

After Christmas dinner, they'd slipped away and driven to the beach to stroll along the nearly deserted white sandy shore. They'd held hands and laughed a lot as they discussed the events of the previous few days.

Noah couldn't have been more shocked when Julie suggested they get married on New Year's Eve. He'd stopped walking and asked, "You're kidding, right?"

She'd looked offended. "I wouldn't joke about something this important."

"But. . . There are so many decisions to be made."

"And we'll make them," Julie promised. "Together. With God's help. He has already answered so many prayers for me. I'm ready to be here with you. Not halfway across the country."

"You can't just up and relocate without preparation," Noah objected.

"I am prepared," Julie said quickly.

Her response had puzzled him. "But surely you've dreamed about your wedding day."

"I have," Julie agreed with a confident nod. "I know exactly what I want."

"Your church?"

She shook her head. "Since I'm marrying Cornerstone's associate pastor and I expect my brother to be at our wedding, it would hardly be fair to the congregation to drag you both away. We can get married at your church. Joey can give me away and conduct the ceremony. Mari and the kids will be my attendants."

"What about a dress?" Noah threw out. "That takes forever."

"I always planned to wear my mother's dress. It's stored in Joe's attic."

"It'll need alterations."

Julie shook her head and smiled brightly. "Fits perfectly. I got my height from Mom."

"What about decorations?"

"The church is already beautifully decorated for Christmas. All I need to do is add a few flowers and it'll be perfect."

"Photographer? They have to be scheduled months in advance."

Julie had refused to be deterred. "There's probably someone at the church. If not, we'll throw some of those disposable cameras around and ask our guests to take our photos."

Noah suspected she'd enjoyed systematically eliminating his every reservation. "What about the reception?"

"We'll have it catered. Surely the congregation won't mind if we provide all the food for the Watch Night service as well."

Noah led her over to a set of wooden steps leading down to the beach. They sat and he'd supported her against his chest, his arm resting about her shoulders. "Julie, you need to slow down. What will Joe think? He requires engaged couples to be counseled prior to marriage."

She'd shrugged. "So he can counsel us. Shouldn't take long considering he knows us so well."

"He may feel he's too close to the situation," Noah said

before asking, "Why the big rush?"

Julie tilted her head back against his shoulder and looked into his eyes. "Because I want next year to be the first of the happiest years of my life and one way I can do that is by marrying the man I love. Do you have any idea how miserable I've been without you? I don't want to spend months planning an event that keeps us separated even longer. If we marry this week, I can go back to Denver to work out my notice, list my condo for sale, pack, and move here before the end of January."

"But we'll still be apart."

"Only for a short time. And then I'll be here as your wife, living with you in our own home, and planning for our future."

The wind off the ocean had picked up and Noah pulled her closer when she shivered. "You could move here anyway. I'm sure Joe would love to have you staying with them."

"I don't want to be a guest in Joe's home," Julie told him. "I want to be your wife."

Despite his uncertainties, Noah hadn't wanted to refuse her. "Can we pray about this?"

"Certainly. But I prayed even before you placed this ring on my finger this morning. I've loved you for a long time, Noah Loughlin. Long enough to believe we can have a good, solid marriage."

"You didn't feel that way two weeks ago."

Julie sighed deeply. "I did. Definitely angry because you left me behind without letting me know how you felt, but I loved you then. I'd hoped you'd propose and if you'd asked, I'd have moved here, too."

"You know I felt I needed to make preparations for the future. I'm still thinking we should consider where we'll be in another year or two."

"You want to wait that long to marry me?" she'd asked, disappointment in her voice.

"I only want what's fair. I'm asking you to give up a lot to be my wife."

"Isn't that the way of every marriage? My dad once told Joey that the secret of a good marriage is both people giving one hundred and fifty percent and expecting nothing in return."

"That's good advice." Noah stood and held out a hand to her. "You're cold. We'd better get back to Joe's. They'll be wondering what happened to us."

Julie smiled at him. "Let's talk to him about the wedding."

Noah shrugged. "Okay, but he's going to agree that it's too soon."

Back at the house, they'd parked and waved at the boys playing with their bikes in the backyard before they went inside. Mari cuddled a sleeping Naomi as she visited with Maggie.

"Where's Joey?" Julie asked softly.

"In the office."

She smiled at her sister-in-law and took Noah's hand, pulling him down the hallway. Julie tapped on the open door. "Do you have a minute?"

He looked up from the computer on his desk. "Sure. You caught me playing with your laptop. I wouldn't mind having one of these."

"It's yours," Julie told him.

"I can't take your computer."

"I bought it for you, Joey. I got a new computer for the church, too."

Joe had looked puzzled. "But you gave me that check for the window. Are you sure you can afford all this?"

"Consider the check my tithes for when I missed church."

"It's very generous of you. It means the church can probably dedicate the Good Shepherd window at Easter."

"Wonderful. I'll look forward to being there to see it."

"You're coming again at Easter?"

"That's what we need to talk to you about, Joe," Noah said, glancing at her before he said, "Julie wants to get married at Cornerstone on New Year's Eve."

Again, Joe looked surprised. "There's plenty of time, Julie."

"No, Joey, there's not. I've spent months of my life angry with God for taking you, Mari, and the kids and then Noah away from me. I buried myself in work, hoping the pain would go away.

"It didn't. I brought that same anger here when I came to stay with the kids and God opened my eyes to the truth. I'm standing in the way of my own happiness. God put it right there before my eyes, but I allowed stubborn pride to blind me. I love Noah and it's important that we spend every moment we have left making each other happy."

"That's an impossibility," Joe told her. "Not every moment."

"Is it?" Julie challenged. "Haven't you always told me nothing is impossible with God?"

Joe couldn't argue with that. "What do you think, Noah?"

"You already know I'd say 'I do' this moment if I could. Julie has ruled out every objection I offered. Tell him your plans," Noah encouraged.

As she'd outlined everything for her brother, Noah couldn't help but feel her excitement. "So you could marry us at seven o'clock with the reception following and still have Watch Night services afterward."

"It could work," Joe had agreed.

"It will," Julie assured. "All I need is for you guys to take the boys for tuxedo fittings. Mari can pick out her dress and something for Naomi and I'll take Mom's dress to the cleaner. If it needs alteration, I'm sure Mari will help. We can be ready with time to spare."

"I'll need to run this by the church board."

"What about counseling?" Noah reminded.

Joe nodded. "It's a requirement."

Julie spoke up. "It's not that I mind the counseling sessions, but I thought they were to make sure the couples are ready for marriage."

"Among other things," Joe agreed. "I want you both to understand the seriousness of the step you're taking."

"Do you trust Noah?" Julie asked.

Joe glanced at him and said, "With my life."

"And your sister? You introduced us. I've known Noah almost as long as you have. I love him with my heart and soul and I want to be with him as his wife as soon as possible. I don't want to spend months planning a major production while living in Colorado. Not when I can be here with the people I love. The only doubts I have relate to the kind of minister's wife I'll be, but I'm willing to give it my all."

Her brother had smiled at them. "We'll set aside some time this week and if you both feel this is right after counseling, I don't see any reason why you can't be married New Year's Eve." Joe stood and held out his hand. "Looks like you'll be getting a tax write-off, buddy."

"Hey, that's the woman of his dreams," Julie said with a laugh.

The days passed in a whirlwind of activity, and as promised, Julie had carried out her plans with time to spare.

Noah suspected Joe's in-depth relationship sessions regarding compatibility, expectations, personalities, communication, conflict resolution, long-term goals, and even intimacy had surprised her. But he'd recognized her sincerity from the questions she asked and the responses she gave.

At the last session, Joe hugged Julie and said, "I wish I could tell you marriage is the easiest thing you'll ever do, but that wouldn't be true. You'll work harder than you've ever worked, but when you celebrate sixty or seventy years together, you'll have no regrets."

Joe had reached out to shake his hand before pulling him into a hug, "Welcome to the family, Noah."

He'd found himself becoming more eager with each passing hour. His parents and family had flown in two days ago. They loved Julie and expressed no doubts as they pitched in to help finalize the plans. His mother had even managed a rehearsal dinner the previous evening.

A couple of Julie's girlfriends had flown in that morning and now sat in a pew on the bride's side of the church as her honorary attendants.

Julie carried a bouquet of the same red roses she'd chosen to blend perfectly with the Christmas decorations. Candles flickered in the low light.

She stopped at his side and when Julie smiled at him, Noah felt at peace. As they had practiced, Joe placed her hand in his and stepped into the pulpit.

"Dearly beloved." The words echoed in the hushed silence of the sanctuary. A few minutes later, everyone laughed when Julie said "I do" and Luke said "I do, too."

After the service, the photographer finished his work and they moved to the fellowship hall to greet their guests. Before they realized it, Joe announced it was time to gather in the sanctuary for Watch Night service.

"Do you want to leave?" Noah asked.

"Let's stay and welcome in the New Year with our church family."

"Come with me," Noah said, leading her to the balcony and their own private world.

They enjoyed the program, particularly the music, and with the New Year only minutes away, Noah lifted her hand to his lips. Her rings sparkled in the light as he whispered, "Look what happened all because you agreed to take care of the kids."

Julie's soft laughter was that of delight. "I was afraid I

couldn't handle them. And now I'm thinking I wouldn't mind being a real Christmas mommy."

Noah grinned at her admission.

The New Year's countdown started and they joined in.

"Three. Two. One. Happy New Year, Mrs. Loughlin!" Noah exclaimed, pulling her into his arms.

Joy sparkled in her eyes as Julie glanced heavenward and whispered, "Thank You, Jesus."

A Letter To Our Readers

Dear Reader:

In order that we might better contribute to your reading enjoyment, we would appreciate your taking a few minutes to respond to the following questions. We welcome your comments and read each form and letter we receive. When completed, please return to the following:

Fiction Editor
Heartsong Presents
PO Box 719
Uhrichsville, Ohio 44683

1. Did you enjoy reading *Christmas Mommy* by Terry Fowler?
   ❑ Very much! I would like to see more books by this author!
   ❑ Moderately. I would have enjoyed it more if

   _____

   _____

   _____

2. Are you a member of **Heartsong Presents**? ❑ Yes ❑ No
   If no, where did you purchase this book? _____

   _____

3. How would you rate, on a scale from 1 (poor) to 5 (superior), the cover design? _____

4. On a scale from 1 (poor) to 10 (superior), please rate the following elements.

   ____ Heroine   ____ Plot
   ____ Hero   ____ Inspirational theme
   ____ Setting   ____ Secondary characters

5. These characters were special because? _____
_____
_____

6. How has this book inspired your life? _____
_____
_____

7. What settings would you like to see covered in future
   Heartsong Presents books? _____
_____
_____

8. What are some inspirational themes you would like to see
   treated in future books? _____
_____
_____

9. Would you be interested in reading other **Heartsong
   Presents** titles? ☐ Yes ☐ No

10. Please check your age range:
    ☐ Under 18   ☐ 18-24
    ☐ 25-34   ☐ 35-45
    ☐ 46-55   ☐ Over 55

Name _____
Occupation _____
Address _____
City, State, Zip_____

KISS

THE

~~COOK~~

Bride

4 stories in 1

When four restaurant owners meet at a trade conference, they discover they have more than just good food in common. Sharing faith, fears, and hopes, they vow to meet again next year. They could each come back, not only with inspirational stories of success and God's guidance, but with a few unexpected guests.

Contemporary, paperback, 368 pages, 5³⁄₁₆" x 8"

_____

Presents